"I'm so sorry

"I'm so sorry, Willow–

They both spoke at the same time.

Willow frowned. "What are you apologizing for, Mike? I'm the one who left you standing at the altar. Was it awful?" she asked. "Did my mother have hysterics?"

"I don't know, because I wasn't there. *I wasn't there,*" Mike repeated.

"What?" Her breath was coming in tiny little gasps as what he was saying finally sank in. "You did it too, didn't you?" She felt almost dizzy with relief. "We both ran out on our wedding!"

Almost at the altar—
will these *nearly*weds become *newly*weds?

Welcome to **Nearlyweds**, our brand-new miniseries
featuring the ultimate romantic occasion—weddings!
Yet these are no ordinary weddings: our beautiful brides
and gorgeous grooms only *nearly* make it to the altar—
before fate intervenes and the wedding's...*off!*

But the story doesn't end there....
Find out what happens in these tantalizingly emotional
novels by some of your best-loved Harlequin Romance®
authors over the coming months.

Look out in May for
The Wedding Secret
by Janelle Denison
#3653

HIS RUNAWAY BRIDE

Liz Fielding

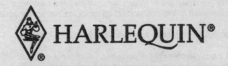

TORONTO • NEW YORK • LONDON
AMSTERDAM • PARIS • SYDNEY • HAMBURG
STOCKHOLM • ATHENS • TOKYO • MILAN • MADRID
PRAGUE • WARSAW • BUDAPEST • AUCKLAND

ISBN 0-373-03645-0

HIS RUNAWAY BRIDE

First North American Publication 2001.

Copyright © 2001 by Liz Fielding.

Visit us at www.eHarlequin.com

Printed in U.S.A.

PROLOGUE

'DON'T go.' Mike kept his arm around her, holding her close. 'I love it when I wake up and you're the first thing I see.'

Willow loved that, too. Loved waking with her cheek pressed against his chest, his arm around her, his corn-coloured hair flopping over his forehead. Loved him. And nestling against him in the dark, his kisses tempting her to stay put and damn the consequences made it hard to be strong.

Getting out of a warm bed to drive home late on a Sunday evening was not top of her 'fun-to-do' list, any more than it was Mike's. Which was why she always found some pressing reason to drive to his place, rather than have him pick her up. With her own car parked outside, she didn't have to make a big deal of it.

'Sorry, sweetheart.' She stirred, kissed him and then forced herself to get out of bed. 'If I stay, I'll have to get up at dawn and dash across town to change for work. Mondays are stressful enough, without that.'

'You should bring a change of clothes with you.' He propped himself up on an elbow and watched her. 'Keep some stuff here. That'd beat the stress.'

It wasn't the first time Mike had suggested this, but Willow was having none of it. She'd handled the toothbrush issue by buying a little travelling set, with a folding toothbrush and a mini tube of toothpaste, easily stored in her capacious shoulder bag, along with a clean pair of knickers and a spare pair of tights. She was a journalist, she reasoned, and had to be prepared for any eventuality. Even on a regional rag like the *Chronicle*.

Leaving clothes at his place was much more serious. The edges of their relationship would become blurred. She'd become too accessible. Before she knew it she'd be there more often than she was at home and he'd be taking her for granted. Expecting her to take on the routine domestic duties because she was there. Because she was female. She'd seen it happen a dozen times.

'It wouldn't help. I have to feed Rasputin and Fang.' She grabbed his bathrobe and headed for the shower. Her two needy goldfish, won by Mike at a visiting fair, were worth their weight in fish food.

'Bring the fish, too,' he called after her. 'I'll build an extension and you can bring your entire collection of cuddly toys, if you like.'

'When I'm here, sweetheart, I prefer to cuddle you.' She turned on the shower and then peered around the bathroom door. 'And an extension would look very peculiar on a second-floor flat.'

He swung himself out of bed, followed her into the bathroom, putting his hand into the water to check the temperature. 'It's the thought that counts.'

'Is that right?'

'You can even bring those horrible wind chimes with the tubes like a church organ.' Then he said, 'Move over. Or had you forgotten about the water-saving campaign you're running in the paper?' This was no way to get home before dawn, Willow thought. But she moved over, hoping to avoid too much tempting physical contact. 'What more can I say?' Mike asked, squeezing some gel into his palm, smoothing it over her back. A whole lot more, she thought, as his hands sapped her will to the point that she had to bite back a groan of pure pleasure. 'Bring everything. Move in here with me.' She held her breath, waiting, but he'd apparently finished. That was it.

She took a slightly shaky breath, turned to face him. 'Why would I want to do that?'

He grinned. 'Because I'm irresistible? Because you hate driving home in the middle of the night, and you're too kind, too tender-hearted to get me out of bed to drive you myself?'

The water was slicking his skin, heating her up. 'You've got that right.'

'Come on. It'll be fun. We can do this all the time.' And he gathered her close, the water cascading over them as he kissed her in a prelude to showing her exactly how much fun it would be.

He was right. He was irresistible. But on this subject she was unshakeable. When he lifted his head, waggled his eyebrows at her, apparently in no doubt as to her answer, she simply sighed and reached for a towel. He wasn't going to allow her to change the subject, not without some explanation. It was time to explain her philosophy on the 'living together' issue.

'Hey,' he complained as she stepped out of the shower stall. 'When I said we should save water, I wasn't thinking drought conditions...'

'Mike, listen to me.' The tone of her voice finally

got through and the grin slipped from his face. He turned off the water, listening. It would help if he wrapped a towel round his waist... 'Darling, you've met my cousin—'

'Crysse? Nice girl. Not a patch on you, but—'

'And you know that Crysse lives with her boyfriend, Sean.'

'People do that these days,' he said, his hands on her shoulders, serious now. Concentration was getting harder by the minute. 'Move in with me. I promise you, no one is going to throw stones at you in the street...' And he kissed her again, moving her gently, but inexorably back towards the bed. It would be so easy to say yes. She wanted to say yes...

Mike's grin was firmly back in place, his grey eyes gleaming with the prospect of success. He clearly thought his case unanswerable.

'No! Listen!' She dug in her heels. Literally and metaphorically. 'Before they lived together, Sean used to take Crysse out all the time. Make a real fuss of her. Every Friday night they went to the cinema, or the theatre. On Saturday they'd go out for the day, or have a meal out at a nice restaurant. On Sunday, he cooked her breakfast and brought it to her in bed. They stayed there most of the day and talked about what they'd do when they were married. How many kids they'd have. Dreaming, you know?'

'Isn't that what we do?' He shrugged. 'Maybe we haven't got around to discussing the number of offspring, but breakfast in bed is a good start. I'll bring you breakfast tomorrow—'

'Then he suggested they move in together.'

'Do it tomorrow. I'll make you breakfast in bed for the rest of your life.'

'That's what Sean said. Crysse was so excited. She sold her flat, redecorated his...'

'I'm beginning to get the uneasy feeling that this story doesn't have a happy ending.'

'That depends on your point of view,' she said. 'Sean's happy. He goes out with his mates on Friday while Crysse, after a hard week attempting to drill the rudiments of mathematics into thirty twelve-year olds, cleans the flat they "share".' She made little quote marks to indicate her doubts about the sharing part. 'These days the highlight of Saturday is a trip to the supermarket while he plays football, or cricket, or whatever other macho pursuit happens to be in season. And on Sunday *she* takes *him* breakfast in bed, where he stays until lunch-time to recover from his exertions on the sports field.'

'And Crysse?'

'Crysse gets on with the ironing. His as well as hers.'

'She should take a break for a while. Let him see what he's missing. She could move into your flat—'

'It doesn't work like that, Mike. What happens is that, while Crysse is proving that she's indispensable to Sean's well-being, some other girl comes along and sees this poor suffering man with no one to iron his shirts for him. It's practically irresistible and she'll come over all motherly. She'll cook and iron and this time, having learned his lesson, Sean will fall over himself to make it permanent.'

He looked at her for a moment, and there was no

trace of a smile as he absorbed the message. 'I take it that's a definite no, then?'

'It's nothing personal. If I was the moving-in kind of girl, there's no one I'd rather move in with than you. But I like my life—'

'And if I make it personal?'

'Please, Mike.' She made a move to collect her clothes, but he blocked her way. 'It's late.'

He remained very still. 'And if I make it personal?' he repeated.

The mood in the flat had changed. Suddenly it was far too intense and Willow felt as if she was balancing on the edge of a precipice that five minutes ago hadn't existed. Her heart flared in panic, she didn't want to lose Mike. She loved him. But before she surrendered the life she had, a life she enjoyed, she had to know he loved her, too. Loved her enough to make a total commitment. No compromise.

'Move in or we break up?' she asked. 'Is that what you're saying?'

'No, angel.' He reached out, cradled her cheek for a moment, then raked his fingers through her short dark curls, holding them back from her forehead so that her face was entirely revealed. 'What I'm saying... What I'm asking...' He seemed to hesitate, consider his words carefully. 'I want you to live with me, Willow Blake. To have you beside me every morning when I wake. To hold you every night as I fall asleep. I guess what I'm saying is, I'm not prepared to risk making Sean's mistake with you. So, how soon can we get married?'

CHAPTER ONE

'I NEED an answer today, Miss Blake, or I can't guarantee—'

'You'll have one!' Willow rang off, then instantly regretted her short temper. It wasn't the builder's fault that she couldn't make up her mind about the cupboards for her new kitchen. That she didn't care a fig for her new kitchen. It was the kitchen out of her worst nightmares, one in which she would be expected to cook three meals a day. Just like her mother...

Why on earth had she ever said she'd marry Mike? Why couldn't she have just moved in with him and settled down to uncomplicated domesticity like her cousin? Crysse was happy, wasn't she? Ironing a few shirts for Mike would have been a lot simpler than living through her mother's idea of the perfect wedding and Mike's father's idea of the perfect house.

It was as if their lives had been taken over by aliens.

Perfectly amiable aliens maybe, but aliens who, in their excitement, their desire to help, had accidentally switched off their 'listening' button. And had clearly never had any kind of grasp of the word 'simple'.

For Willow, a simple wedding conjured up visions of a small country church, a dress from the local bridal shop, standard grey morning suits all round for the men, two bridesmaids. Two grown-up bridesmaids who could be relied upon not to eat their posies, burst into tears, or worse. A simple reception.

Her mother's version of simple involved Melchester Cathedral, scrubbed choirboys in starched-white surplices, massed bell-ringers and a full-scale posse of bridesmaids and page-boys. Add in enough flowers and ribbon to keep a florist in business for a year...

Then there was the reception.

No. She was stressed enough, she absolutely refused to contemplate the reception. Or the vast edifice of the confectioner's art that was her wedding cake. Forget simple. From Willow's perspective her life appeared to be attracting complications in the manner of a magnet confronted with a open box of iron filings.

And the wedding was just the visible, outward sign of 'complicated'. Liveable with. Just. Real complications came in small, less obvious packages. Long white envelopes with the logo of a national newspaper in the corner.

If life was simple, she'd phone the telephone number on the letter in her bag, say, thanks, but no thanks. She was no longer available. They'd left it too late to offer her the job of her dreams. She was getting married on Saturday. She'd phone and she'd say all that and she wouldn't be able to stop herself from grinning while she said it. But she kept putting it off.

Which was why it was so complicated.

'Are you all right, Willow?'

'What?' She started, realising that Emily Wootton was staring at her with concern. 'Oh, yes. It's nothing.' And she lifted her shoulders in what she hoped was a convincing shrug. 'I'm getting married on Saturday—'

'Really?' The older woman smiled. 'How lovely.'

Willow had her doubts. 'I'm sure everyone else will enjoy themselves. I'm just looking forward to next week when I'll be on a beach in St Lucia and the last few weeks will be nothing but a blur.' She made a big effort at a smile. 'You were telling me about these cottages the Trust has been given by the Kavanaghs?' she invited, before she broke down and poured out her misgivings to a woman she'd only met a couple of times. But who else was there? No one who knew Mike and had seen the house, could be expected to understand; she didn't understand herself. If she could just go back to the night he'd proposed, hear him say it again. Convince herself that he really meant it. He'd seemed so distracted lately... 'You need money to convert them into a holiday home for deprived children, is that it?'

'No, that's all done. All that's left is the decorating and we're looking for volunteers to help out.' She grinned. 'I don't suppose I can tempt you to change your honeymoon plans? I mean who *really* wants to go to the West Indies?' A great fat tear escaped and slid down Willow's cheek. 'Willow?' She wanted to put her head down on her desk and howl. 'Willow, dear, is there anything I can do?'

'No.' She sniffed, searching her pocket for a tissue. 'It's just pre-wedding nerves.' Probably. Pre-wedding nerves and the strain of trying very hard not to let anyone see that she'd fallen in hate at first sight with the house Mike's parents had bought for them as a wedding present. A huge red-brick edifice with five

bedrooms, three bathrooms and half an acre of land-
scaped garden that would take every minute she could
spare from cooking and dusting to keep it from re-
verting to wilderness.

She and Mike hadn't come to any decision about
where they'd live. His flat or hers. They were both
convenient, easy to run, perfect for a busy couple.
Then—whammy. An invitation to lunch from Mike's
parents at a country pub with a route that just happened to bypass the house from hell. The kind of
house that needed a full-time wife, not a woman with
a life of her own and a career that was about to take
off into the stratosphere. Or would be, if she wasn't
getting married.

It was becoming clear that as Mike's wife she
wouldn't have a life of her own.

No more Willow Blake. She'd be Mrs Michael
Armstrong, consort to Michael Armstrong, newspaper
proprietor. In the fullness of time she'd become
mother to the statutory two-point-four children, with
a busy life as a champion of local good causes and
all-round pillar-of-the-community. In ten years she'd
have turned into every woman's worst nightmare, a
carbon copy of her mother.

Oh, she'd carry on working for a while—quietly
shunted off into the more ladylike stuff, the WI meet-
ings, the garden club, local celebrities. Just until the
babies came along. That house demanded babies to
fill its echoing spaces. Mike's father was already re-
ferring to bedroom number two as 'the nursery'. As
if the Peter Rabbit decor wasn't enough of a hint.

As for Mike, well she didn't know what he was

thinking any more. Suddenly he was more distant than the Khyber Pass.

Which was why the letter offering her the job of her dreams was still in her bag, still unanswered. A lifeline.

'It's, er, rather a big house, Mike. Not quite your usual style. A bit different from the hayloft,' Cal pressed anxiously.

'That depends on your view of big.' Michael Armstrong was eager to cut off any discussion about what his usual style entailed. Cal was his oldest friend, his best man, and he knew him far too well to be easily fooled. 'Willow was brought up in a ten-bedroom mansion.'

Mike had been working up to taking her to Maybridge, gauging her reaction to an alternative life-style; her excitement over the house had made him realise that it was going to be a non-starter.

'Right. Well, I suppose if you're both happy with it, that's all that matters.' Cal clearly wasn't convinced, but let it drop. 'When are you supposed to be moving in?'

Mike dragged himself back from some place where he wasn't expected to live to this monstrosity of a house which his father, with all his plans apparently about to be fulfilled, had sprung on them as a wedding present. There had been no prior consultation because his father had known what his answer would be. The cunning old fox had relied on Willow to do his dirty work for him. And since she'd clearly loved the place, he'd choked back the 'thanks, but no thanks'. There was no way he could refuse it.

Realising that Cal was regarding him with a look that suggested his face was betraying his innermost thoughts, Mike quickly answered, 'The house is supposed to be ready when we get back from honeymoon.'

'You don't sound…' his friend hesitated as he sought for the appropriate word '…optimistic.' Mike ignored the underlying invitation to say what he really felt and kept quiet. 'Ookaaay.' Cal stretched out the vowels in acknowledgement that, as a topic of conversation, it was going no further. 'I'm sure you and Willow can live without carpet for a week or two. And there's no hurry to furnish the nursery,' he added, in an attempt to lighten the atmosphere, gesturing at the giveaway decor of the second bedroom. 'Unless there's something you're not telling me? It would certainly explain the prodigal's unexpected return to the fold—'

'My father's trip to intensive care provoked my return,' Mike declared. 'It was never my intention to stay in Melchester.'

'Until you met Willow.' *Until he met Willow.* 'Does she know how you feel about stepping into your father's shoes? I only ask because when we were having a drink last week, I got the distinct impression that she thinks you're taking the fast route to businessman of the year.' He waited. 'That you've got accountants' ink running through your veins.' Then he added, 'She doesn't know about Maybridge, does she? You haven't told her.'

'Mind your own business, Cal.'

'I'm your best man. This is my business.'

'You've met her. She's old money, centuries-deep

breeding.' Mike's gesture conveyed unspoken volumes. 'She was simply marking time, doing the social stuff at the newspaper until one of the local chinless wonders invited her to become his Lady Chinless Wonder and breed little chinless wonders.'

'Excuse me? Have you actually read any of the stuff she writes? Listened—'

'I have to live with the *Chronicle*, Cal. I'm not prepared to sleep with it.' He held up his hands. 'Okay, okay. If there was a prize for writing up the gardening club's committee meeting I'm sure she'd get it. But you can understand why I haven't suggested she move in over my workshop in Maybridge and live off what I make with my hands.'

'What you wouldn't do for your father, you'll do for love? In your shoes, I have to admit I'd do the same.' He looked around, then grinned. 'Maybe the nursery should be a priority after all.'

'This is my father's idea of a subtle hint. He could give a steam hammer lessons.'

'The heart attack hasn't slowed him down?'

'Heart attack? I'm beginning to suspect that it was nothing more serious than a bad bout of indigestion.' But it had done the trick. Brought him racing home, full of guilt, to take over managing the *Chronicle* and its sister magazine, the *Country Chronicle* while his mother took the old man on holiday. A long holiday. He should have run then, smelt a rat the moment his holiday-hating father hadn't objected to a six-week cruise. 'I don't know. Maybe I'm just being cynical. Whatever, it's reminded him of his own mortality.' He gestured at the wallpaper. 'Hence the rabbits.'

'That's it? No other problems?'

Mike dragged his fingers through his hair. 'Well, I have to get my hair cut before Saturday,' he said, making a determined effort to shake off a sense of doom.

He loved Willow. She'd been the one bright spark in the darkness when he'd been forced to come home, take up the reins of the family business while his father convalesced.

He'd walked into the office that first morning, his mood as black as the *Chronicle's* headlines when she'd cannoned into him, her belongings scattering across the floor. She'd dived after her phone to check that it wasn't damaged before rounding on him with a sharp, 'Why don't you look where you're going?'

About to put her right about who hadn't been looking, he'd caught his breath and there had a been a small, still moment when everything, including his heart, had seemed to stop. Then she'd grinned and said, 'Oops. Bad mistake. Memo to brain. Don't yell at your new boss until you've been properly introduced.' When he'd continued to stare at her, his tongue apparently stuck to the roof of his mouth, she'd added, 'You *are* Michael Armstrong? There's a photograph of you on your father's desk—'

'It's Mike,' he'd said. 'And I'm not the boss. Just standing in his shoes for a couple of weeks.'

'Oh well, hello, Mike.' She'd stuck out her hand. 'I'm Willow Blake.' Then she'd given a little yelp. 'And I'm late.' And then he'd been watching her run for her car with a smile on his face that would have given the Cheshire cat an inferiority complex.

He hadn't intended more than a flirtation. A brief dalliance. Nothing heavy, nothing serious. She'd taken some catching, had kept him at arm's length for longer than he was used to. The chase had been fun, though, and catching her had been…well…as if he'd found something he hadn't known he'd been missing. But he'd pursued her as Michael Armstrong, acting head of the company she worked for. She was a class act and he'd needed every advantage he could use to stack the scales in his favour.

And when he'd caught her there didn't seem to be any particular hurry to explain that this was just a temporary persona. Then he'd asked her to marry him.

And had meant it.

Her slightly stunned 'yes', had left him wanting to shout *stop the presses…reset the front page…I've got some real news…*—drowning out the small warning voice telling him that she thought she was getting the heir to a publishing empire. Not a man who, in his real life, lived in the old hayloft above what had once been a coach house and stables. Above his workshop where he lived an entirely different dream.

Could it be that he was afraid she wouldn't want the real Michael Armstrong? Was that why he'd put off telling her?

Once his father had driven them out to the house, handed them the estate agent's glossy brochure, gift-wrapped, it had been too late.

'You only have one life, Mike,' Cal said, interrupting his black thoughts, reading his mind with frightening accuracy. 'You have to live your own dream.' Then, frowning, he said, 'It's the bride who's supposed to be having last-minute nerves.'

'I'd advise you to wait until you try it from the

business end of the wedding banns before you make such sweeping judgements.'

'That sounds like a bad case of cold feet.'

The inflection in Cal's voice again urged him to confide his misgivings, but things had gone too far for that, so he shook his head. 'I guess I thought it would be simpler. I guess I thought getting married was just a question of turning up at the church on time and not losing the ring.'

'You can safely leave those details to me. As for the rest...' He glanced at his watch. 'It's nearly lunch time. Why don't you go and find the lovely Willow, give yourselves the afternoon off and remind yourself what this is all about?'

'I haven't got time.' Cal's brows rose slightly. 'I'll be away from the business for the best part of a month.' Except it wasn't going to be *the* business, any more. It was going to be *his* business. He'd conformed, settled down and his father was all set to hand over the minute the ink was dry on the marriage register.

'Mike?' She'd been waiting an hour for him, finishing the feature about the holiday cottages, tidying up loose ends. Thinking of some way to tell him about the job she'd been offered.

Leaving the paper would be bad enough, a kick in the teeth of both Mike and his father. And she'd have to travel to London every day, not always making it home, maybe. It was possible that if the *Globe* knew she was about to get married, they might not be so keen to have her...

Mike finally made a note in the margin of a column of figures, then looked up.

'What is it, Willow?'

She looked at the pencil keeping his place in the margin and said, 'Nothing. Absolutely nothing.'

She didn't wait for his response, but walked quickly out of the building. Her car was in for a service and Mike had offered to give her a lift to Crysse's. He'd clearly forgotten and she'd rather walk than interrupt his love affair with a calculator. That was what you got for falling in love with an accountant.

She hoisted her shoulder bag a little higher. She'd walk off the bad day with the builders, the endless queries from her mother about details, details, details. She no longer cared about the colour of the ribbons on the pew ends, or whether there would be sufficient roses in the garden for buttonholes. In a world where there were children who'd never had a holiday, never would have a holiday unless someone like Emily Wootton made it possible, such things didn't rate a second thought.

But walking was a mistake. She was wearing new shoes and, by the time she'd gone half a mile, the deceptively soft leather had raised a blister on her heel. If she limped up the aisle, every painful step captured on video for posterity, her mother would probably kill her. Which would solve every one of her problems at a stroke. The other option was to catch a bus. As she reached a stop, she joined the queue, eased the weight off her foot and waited.

'Offer you a lift, lady?' She forced herself to ignore the little heart-lift as Mike pulled up beside her, an unruly cow-lick of honey-coloured hair sliding over his forehead as he leaned across to push open the passenger door of his black four-wheel drive.

'My mother told me never to take lifts from strangers,' she said, horribly conscious of the envious glances of women with heavy shopping bags. Then she said, 'I thought you were busy.'

'I was. I am. And I have a headache to end all headaches, which is why I forgot about giving you a lift to Crysse's.'

'I hope your stag night was worth the headache.'

'Nothing is worth this amount of pain.' And it hadn't worked. No amount of alcohol or the juvenile high jinks organised by Cal, had been able to blot out the mess he'd got himself into. He glanced at the queue of people who had stopped straining to see if a bus was coming and were now all watching their little drama. 'Please get in, Willow.'

'How did you know I didn't call a taxi?' She considered taking out her phone and doing just that.

'You were angry.' And he didn't blame her. 'In your shoes I'd have walked.'

'Then, you'd have made a mistake.' Willow was attracting more attention than she cared for. And calling a taxi would be petty. She took a deep breath and climbed in beside him. Shut the door. 'My shoes have given me a blister.'

'Oh, hell. Come here.' Mike forgot all about the bus queue as he put his arms around her and she went to his shoulder like a kitten to a warm blanket. 'I'm sorry.' He eased back, looked down at her, took the full force of her electric blue eyes and found himself wishing he'd heeded Cal's advice, taken yesterday afternoon off and stayed in bed. Until this morning. 'Do you have to go to Crysse's this evening?'

'I'm afraid so. There's the crèche at the reception to be finalised, a panic about a torn bridesmaid dress, some place names still need to be written—' She was ticking the endless list off on her fingers, but he caught her hand, stopping her.

'Do you know something?'

'What?'

'If I'd known then, what I know now, I would never have asked you to marry me.'

'Believe me,' she came back without hesitation, 'if I'd known then what I know now, I'd have said no.' And for just a second something flickered in the depths of her eyes. Almost, he'd have said, as if she meant it. Then she shivered. 'I'm getting through by dealing with it the way I would an overdue trip to the dentist. Agony at the time, but afterwards...'

Her voice trailed off, leaving him to fill in the blank with something appropriate, like 'bliss', he thought. Instead he said, 'Hold onto that thought,' as he released her. 'And buckle up.' He engaged gear and turned to check the oncoming traffic.

Anything rather than face the everlasting afterwards behind a desk, in an office, balancing the books.

'I've been offered a job, Crysse.'

'A job? What kind of job?' Her cousin looked up from repairing the hem that one of the tiny bridesmaids had somehow managed to put her foot through. 'Surely the *Evening Post* isn't trying to poach you? What a nerve!' She slipped in another pin. 'Although, come to think of it, maybe working with your husband isn't that great an idea. Twenty-four hours a day of perfect bliss might be more than any ordinary woman could stand. Not that I'm in any position to judge.'

'I scarcely see Mike at the office. Besides, it isn't with the *Post*. I couldn't work for a rival paper.' Crysse looked up from threading a needle. 'You remember I applied for a job on the *Globe*?'

'The *Globe*? But that was months ago. Last year. Before you met Mike. I thought they said they weren't interested.'

'Not exactly. They said they'd let me know. Well, now they have. It seems they've been making changes. Appointed a new editor, going tabloid. They're putting a women's supplement in their Friday edition and they want me to join the team.'

Crysse jabbed the needle into the cream silk. 'I bet your bread never falls butter-side down, either, does it?'

'What?'

'Nothing.' She continued picking up the hem with neat little stitches. 'Forget I said that. Congratulations.'

'Crysse?' She shook her head. 'What is it?'

'Nothing.' Then she shrugged. 'Everything. I'm pea-green jealous if you must know.'

'Jealous?'

'I know, I know. It's horrible of me, but I can't help it.' Her cheeks heated up. 'You've got everything. The full set. A man any woman would die for—a man who actually believes in marriage, a wedding that's going to be featured in the *Country*

Chronicle, a fabulous new house courtesy of your fa-ther-in-law and all I've heard all evening is you whin-ing on about how irritating it is to be constantly both-ered about the colour of ribbons, and flowers and all those other tedious little decisions that the harassed bride has to cope with. Anyone would think you didn't really want to marry Mike.'

'No...' Well, maybe she had been letting off steam, hoping that Crysse would turn it all around, make her laugh, see the funny side of it all, see it straight, the way she usually did. 'I wasn't whining. Was I?'

'Big time. And now, as if the icing on your partic-ular cake wasn't already thick enough, you've landed the job of your dreams.' Willow watched in horror as twin tears welled up in her cousin's eyes and ran un-checked to drip onto the elaborate little dress she was stitching. 'What have I got, hmm? I've been with Sean for five years—*five years* and he's further from marrying me now than he ever was. I'm nearly thirty and I want a proper home, Willow. A house with a garden. I want babies—'

'Oh, Crysse!' Willow dropped her pen and reached out for her, holding her tightly as she let go of her feelings and broke her heart. 'Have you talked to Sean? You can't go on like this. You have to tell him how you feel.'

She sounded like the weekly advice column in the Chronicle. *Talk to your partner. Explain your con-cerns about your relationship.*

Agony Aunt heal thyself.

'What's the point? Why should he make the effort when he's got everything he wants right now? I should have been like you, Willow. You knew what you wanted and stuck out for it. You always were the clever one. You never would settle for second best.'

She considered admitting that she'd spent the last couple of weeks wishing she'd just moved in with Mike when he'd asked her. But, in her present fragile state, Crysse would probably believe she was being patronised. Better try to be positive. 'Okay. So if you don't want what you've got, maybe it's time to ask yourself what you *do* want. Hmm?'

Crysse rubbed her palms over her cheeks. 'I thought I wanted this. I settled for this. But it's not enough.'

'Then, dump the ungrateful wretch. You've wasted enough time washing socks for a man whose idea of commitment is supporting Melchester Rovers when they play at home. Do something you really want with your life, before it's too late.'

'It takes a lot of courage to walk away from five years together, Willow. It's like a divorce. No lawyers, no paperwork, but it's still dismantling your life, starting over again, five years older and not quite so dewy fresh.' Crysse sniffed, took the tissue Willow offered and blew her nose. 'What about you?' she said, with forced brightness. 'What does Mike think about this job you've been offered?'

Crysse firmly changed the subject, clearly not wanting to discuss changing her life. She didn't want to change her life, she just wanted Sean to shape up and change his.

'I haven't told him yet,' Willow said, letting it go. 'I haven't told anyone but you.'

Crysse's eyebrows rose a fraction. 'Don't you think you should?'

'I was hoping for some words of wisdom from my favourite cousin.'

'It sounds to me as if you were hoping I'd say you can have your cake and eat it, too.'

'Don't mince your words, darling,' she said, a touch wryly. 'Feel free to say exactly what you think.'

'What I think, *darling*, is that Mike's life is here, in Melchester. And that house you're moving into suggests he's expecting a full-time wife with her mind on nothing in the immediate future but family planning. You *are* getting married on Saturday, remember?' Crysse, the space between her eyes wrinkled in a searching little frown, suddenly reached out and took her hand. 'That is what *you* really want, isn't it?'

Did she? Want that? The home and the babies... She loved Mike, but the prospect of writing 'housewife and mother' in the occupation slot of life hadn't obliterated her other dream. The one where she would have her own byline in a national newspaper before she was thirty.

The letter from the *Globe* was offering her that. Once she was established she could freelance, but first she needed to make a name for herself.

Surely Mike would understand.

Of course he would.

He looked up as she eased herself into the chair on the visitor side of his desk. She propped her elbows on the desk and said, 'Can I buy you lunch, boss?'

He leaned back, grinned at her. 'Do you really want to eat?'

'You choose. I've got half an hour before a session

of hell at the hairdresser, so it's a sandwich in the pub, or we can lock the door, draw the blinds—'

'It may come to that. I've scarcely seen outside the office all week.'

'You're opting for the sandwich?'

He rose, came round the desk and took her hand. 'Call me pathetic, but the idea of making love to you with the entire staff exchanging knowing looks on the other side of the door isn't my idea of a good time.'

'You're no fun now you're officially the boss, do you know that?'

'No kidding?' he said, as they crossed the road to the pub. 'Well, it's not official until we get back from St Lucia. Maybe I should resign now.'

'That's my line,' she said, jumping at the opening he'd given her. 'I've been offered another job and unless I start getting some serious perks as your number one reporter, I might just take it.' The words came out in rush, but they came out. She'd said it. It wasn't so difficult. But she kept her gaze fixed on the board above the bar. 'A ploughman's and a tomato juice, please, George,' she said to the barman. An ominous silence from Mike forced her to turn and face the music.

'What job?'

'Make that for two, George.' She paid for their lunch and headed for a table near the window.

'What job?'

This was it. No going back. Too late to wish she'd just written back to say thanks, but no thanks. 'The *Globe* have offered me a job.'

'The *Globe*?' He seemed to be searching for a

cross-match in his memory bank. She could see the exact moment when he connected. The shock. 'You don't mean The *Globe* in London?' He frowned. 'Isn't that a bit...' She lifted her brows, inviting him to finish. 'Downmarket for someone like you?'

What the heck did that mean? Like her? 'It's a national daily with a circulation of millions.' He said nothing. 'You're supposed to be impressed.'

'Okay. I'm impressed,' he said, after a pause in which the world turned. 'Would you have taken it?'

'Would?' His calm assumption that she wouldn't be taking the job without even discussing the possibility, without discussing how they might handle it so that it would be possible, seriously irritated her. 'You don't think I should?'

'Not unless you're planning to move to London and save married life for the weekends.' Then he added, 'Are you?'

'I could commute.' She checked his expression. It was totally blank. 'No?' Still nothing. Her decision. No help, no encouragement. 'Oh, well, I'll ring Toby Townsend this afternoon and tell him.'

'When did you apply for this job?'

'Months ago. I had an interview but nothing came of it.' She gave an awkward little shrug. 'That is, until Toby's letter arrived on Monday.' George brought their lunch, launching into a long complaint against the new parking restrictions that were killing his business, demanding to know why the paper wasn't doing something about it. Somehow, after that, the subject of the job offer never cropped up again.

Later, back in the office, she told herself that Mike

was right. Probably. No, absolutely. It was impossible. Stupid to even imagine… She'd ring and tell them that she was no longer available. It was fine. She loved Mike. She was going to marry him. But a little niggle at the back of her mind kept saying that if she hadn't pushed it, hadn't pushed him into proposing, she could have had it all. A career in the week, Mike at the weekends. A girlfriend could do that but being a wife meant compromise. Being a wife was a full-time job.

She punched in the number before she could weaken again. Toby Townsend wasn't in the office, she was told. She should phone on Monday. Explanations were beyond her. She'd write. Composed the letter in her head while the hairdresser snipped at her hair, teasing at it until her bridal coronet sat perfectly in a nest of curls. Typed it as soon as she got back to the office, putting it into her bag to post later. Then she went in search of Mike, needing to have him hold her, reassure her that she was doing the right thing.

But he'd left the office right after lunch and his secretary didn't know where he'd gone. Just that he wasn't expected back.

Willow took out her cellphone. Tapped in the text message, *'Where are you? Can we meet?'* He used to do that all the time when they'd first started dating. When she was out in the sticks covering some local event. She'd reply with something like, *'If you can find me, you can buy me dinner.'* All he had to do was check the editorial diary and he was always there, waiting for her. It seemed like a century ago. A different life.

She looked at the message she'd keyed in. She couldn't begin to guess where he'd be. So she cancelled it.

Mike opened up the big double doors of his workshop, letting in the light. There were plans tacked up on the far wall. Long lengths of beautiful hardwoods filled the racks. A small table, finished but for the final polishing, stood on the workbench, abandoned when he'd got a call to say that his father had been taken ill.

He'd woken up with it on his mind. Unfinished business. Something that had to be completed before he could finally shut the doors on that part of his life. Before he called the letting agent and told them to look for a tenant.

He peeled off his jacket, tugged at his tie, stripped off the formal shirt, shedding the invisible shackles for half a day. There was an old work shirt hanging on a peg and, as he pulled it over his head, it felt like coming home.

He walked around the deceptively simple piece of furniture, remembering the way the design had formed in his head, the satisfaction as his hands had turned the line on the paper into reality.

He'd give it to Willow. He wouldn't tell her he'd made it, but every time he saw it he would know that he had once been more than a man who pushed numbers around on a balance sheet.

Mike was outside her flat when she got home. 'More presents?' he said as she opened up the back of the car.

'My mother rang, that's why I'm so late. Where have you been?' She looked up as he took her bag. 'You smell as if you've been hugging trees.'

'Close,' he said. 'I've brought you a present, too. A piece of furniture.' He opened the rear of the four-by-four, took out something wrapped in sheeting and carried it up to her flat. 'Well, go on. You can look.'

She pulled off the sheet and caught her breath. It was a small table, stunningly modern, timeless in its simplicity. 'Oh, Mike! This is so beautiful!' She touched the surface, ran her fingers over it. 'It's like silk. What wood is this?'

'Cherry.'

'It's…' She lifted her shoulders, lost for the right word to adequately convey her appreciation. 'I can't explain it.' She glanced up at him. 'It looks as if it should be in a museum. Does that sound silly?'

Mike's fingers slid over the polished surface. Some of his early pieces had become collectors' items, sold on, displayed, too precious to be used. He hated that. 'It was made to be used, not looked at.' He wanted his furniture to take on the patina of everyday wear and tear, to absorb history.

'Where did you get it?'

'I… It was designed…made by someone I know.'

'Really? Is he coming to the wedding? Can I meet him? Maybe we could run a feature in *Country Chronicle*—'

'No, Willow. This is his last piece. He's closed his workshop. It's not a business for a family man.'

'That's sad—'

'That's life,' he said abruptly. 'What have you got there?' He picked up a box. 'A juicer? Does this mean I'm going to be getting fresh orange juice every morning for breakfast?'

She swallowed. Was that it? The highlight of her life from now on? Juicing oranges for Mike? 'It's from Josie,' she said, ducking the question. 'I went to school with her. She's a bit of a health-food freak, juices everything. Carrots. Celery. You name it, she drinks it.'

'Well,' he said. 'That sounds…great.'

Was it great? Or was it just easier to go through with the wedding than walk away, easier than packing up the juicer and saying, sorry, this isn't for me. Was she, like Crysse, going on because the alternative was just so messy, too painful to contemplate?

She was good at telling other people what was good for them, but what about her? And Mike?

Her ghostly reflection stared back at her from the car window. On the surface, everything was perfect. Her dress, her hair, her make-up.

'Nearly there, Willow. All set?'

She turned to her father, distinguished in his morning suit, his top hat resting on his lap as the car, ribbons fluttering, drove in slow state towards a church filled with friends and family, all gathered for her big day. What would they do, she wondered, if she didn't turn up?

'Did you wonder *before* you married Mum whether you were making a terrible mistake?'

'It's a big step. Nerves are to be expected.' Then her father frowned. 'Or is there something more?'

'I don't know. Maybe.' Then she said, 'If I hadn't been offered that wretched job...'

The letter to Toby Townsend lay on the hall table. She'd kept putting off posting it. She'd meant to do it last night, along with the thank-you letters for wedding presents like the juicer and the clock to count the hours that she'd spend dusting a house she'd loathed on sight.

She'd had to smile and smile to keep her feelings bottled up, so as not to hurt Mike's father. Not to hurt Mike, who'd been so overwhelmed by the generosity of the gift of the house that he'd been quite lost for words. And somehow the letter hadn't quite made it into the box.

'Tell me, Willow, if Mike had rung last night and said, ''Let's forget the wedding,'' how would you have felt?'

'Relieved.' The word, blurted out without hesitation, shocked her. She said it again. 'Relieved.' And this time she knew it was true. Not because she didn't love Mike, but because she didn't want this life. As the car, approaching the church, began to slow she said, 'Don't stop!'

The driver grinned. 'You girls do like to make a man suffer. Once more round the block is it?'

'Yes, once more round the block. Dad, I can't do this to Mike. Can I? He's in the church now, waiting for me—'

'If you're really that unsure, my dear, then I think you must.'

'Mother will never forgive me.'

'This has nothing to do with your mother. This is *your* life.'

'But the reception—'

'It won't be wasted. People will still need to eat.'

Was that the only reason she was going through with this? Concern about wasting some food, upsetting her mother? 'Tell Mike—' She stopped. What? That she loved him? That she loved him but she couldn't marry him? Better to say nothing...

'Leave it to me, sweetheart.' He squeezed her hand. 'Drop me off at the corner, driver, and then take my daughter home.' He got out, held the door for a moment. 'Willow, about your mother... Maybe it *would* be a good idea to disappear for a few days.'

Was that why he was doing it? Going through with the wedding? Taking on the *Chronicle*? Not to disappoint his father nor the Josies of this world? One life, Cal had said. He had one shot at getting it right. He didn't have time to waste it living other people's dreams.

And Willow? What about Willow? Mike loved her. She was the best thing that had happened to him in years, but she wanted a career. He wasn't stupid. She'd been aching for him to say she should take that job at the *Globe*.

He'd seen it and part of him had wanted to say, go for it, don't waste a minute of your life. But there was another, darker side that was all screwed up, that reminded him that *she* was the one who'd insisted on marriage. Well, she'd got it. She couldn't have it all.

What kind of start was that? How soon before they'd both be wishing they were somewhere else?

Out of sight someone was playing the organ, quiet incidental music, a counterpoint to the quiet rustling as the wedding guests took their places, exotic hats surreptitiously angled as women glanced sideways at him, tipping close as they whispered to each other.

The sun was shining in through the stained glass, spattering the marble steps with red and blue and gold. But he felt cold and the scent of flowers in the vast arrangements either side of the aisle was making him feel slightly nauseous.

How much longer? He glanced at his watch. Willow was late. Last minute nerves? Suppose she didn't turn up? How would he feel? Devastated or just relieved?

'Don't look so worried, Mike, I haven't lost the rings.'

Relieved.

'Cal, what would you say if I told you I don't want to do this?'

Cal looked at him as if he was about to say something flippant, then he frowned. 'Is that a serious question?' His face must have been answer enough, because he said, 'For the last week you've looked like a man on the way to the gallows. I thought it was the *Chronicle*—'

'It was. That and Josie's juicer.'

'What has a juicer got to do with it?' Cal waited, but when no further explanation was forthcoming he took in a deep breath. 'You'd better make up your mind what you want, Mike. The minute Willow steps foot in this church you're committed.'

'I'm already committed. I can't—'

'For heaven's sake, if you've got real doubts you must get out of here. Now.'

'Tell her...' What? What could he possibly say? That he loved her but that this life was not the one he'd ever wanted to live? 'Tell her father that I'll pay for all this...'

'Sure. Now go. I've got things to do.'

CHAPTER TWO

WHAT had he done? What on earth had he done?

Mike drove, not caring where, just as long he got away from Melchester, responding to the heavy traffic on automatic, not really seeing the cars, or the trucks, not seeing anything but Willow arriving at the church in her beribboned car expecting him to be waiting for her, ready to pledge his life to her. She'd been prepared to give up the job of her dreams for him. And he wasn't there.

He dragged his hand over his face feeling sick and heartsore, stunned at the unhappiness he'd caused because he wouldn't, couldn't live the life expected of him from the moment of his birth.

At least that was no longer an issue. His father had probably denounced him from the pulpit. Publicly disowned him. If he returned to Melchester any time within the next ten years he'd probably be lynched.

He'd have to write her. Try to explain. What? That he wasn't the man she thought he was? That his father had seized on their marriage and used it as an opportunity to pin him down, turn him into a mirror image of himself?

How could he expect Willow to understand how the thought of that sucked the very life out of him? He should have told her, right at the start. But he hadn't intended a flirtatious game of kiss-chase to turn into a lifetime commitment. Hadn't expected to be sandbagged by love.

And now it was too late for explanations. Far better to walk away. Have her loathe him rather than try to understand him. To risk her feeling even the faintest touch of guilt when what had happened was entirely his fault.

It was over. Finished. Now all he had to do was disappear while the dust settled. But first he needed coffee, needed to eat something, or he'd pass out at the wheel.

The motorway was packed with cars, roof-racks piled high with suitcases, as holiday-makers returned to London. Willow tried not to think about her honeymoon suitcase, packed and waiting at the hotel where she and Mike were to have had their reception, then spend their wedding night. A suitcase packed with swimwear, the lovely evening dresses and sexy underwear she and Crysse had chosen during a giggly, girly visit to London right after Mike had slipped a diamond ring on her finger. Right after the formal portrait of the pair of them appeared in the *Country Chronicle*, with the announcement of their forthcoming marriage.

She glanced at her left hand resting on the steering wheel. It looked naked.

A sign flashed by with those little life-saving icons, a cup and a knife and fork. With relief, she indicated and pulled off. She was on the point of a brilliant career. Not the time to have an accident because visibility was compromised by a totally irrational desire to weep.

The car park was packed with more holiday-
makers. She didn't want to push her way into the
restaurant, fight to be served. But she needed to eat.
She hadn't been able to face more than a mouthful of
cereal and, as for lunch…well, lunch was to have
been one of those once-in-a-lifetime affairs with witty
speeches and many toasts to happy-ever-after while
the staff photographer took pictures for the colour
spread that would appear in the *Chronicle*'s magazine. She gulped and reached for the box of man-
sized tissues she kept in her car.

She'd thrown jeans, T-shirts, underwear of the
plain, serviceable variety into a zip-up bag for her
flight from Melchester. Not what she'd planned to be
wearing today.

The handful of extra-strength tissues to mop up the
deluge of tears weren't part of her trousseau, either.
Today all she'd anticipated needing was a small lacy
thing, bridal-issue, perfect for dabbing away tears of
happiness.

She groaned and laid her head on the back of hands
as they grasped the steering wheel and thought about
what she'd done. Seeing Mike, in her mind's eye,
standing at the altar, waiting for her. Turning as her
father appeared in the church doorway.

Alone.

How on earth could she have done that to a man
she loved? Put him through the ultimate in public
humiliation?

What would he say? Do? Cal would get him out
of the church…

The church. All those people. The buzz of excited
gossip. Willow groaned again. Her father hadn't ut-

tered a word of reproach but her mother wouldn't be
that restrained.

And what on earth would happen to the three tiers
of confection that she and Mike should have been
cutting with a silver-handled knife engraved with
their names and the date?

'Are you all right, miss?'

She looked up. It was a uniformed man from one
of the motoring organisations. Unfortunately it would
take more than a spanner to put this mess right. 'Yes,'
she said. 'Yes, I'm fine. I just need a cup of coffee.'

'Have something to eat, too. And take a nap if
you're tired. You don't need to get anywhere so
quickly that it's worth taking risks.'

'It's all right. Really. I'm in no hurry.' She had
nowhere to hurry to, nobody waiting. Then, because
he didn't look convinced, she said, 'I'll get a sandwich, I promise.'

Reassured he returned to his stand and she crossed
the crowded car park, joined the anonymity of the
jostling mass in the ladies' room, cleaned up her face,
removing the elaborate make-up that looked horribly
inappropriate with jeans, dragging her fingers through
her hair determined to ruffle up the perfection of her
early morning styling. Trying to distance herself from
the bride she was supposed to be.

How on earth was she going to get through the next
four weeks until she joined the *Globe*? What was she
going to do? She couldn't face her mother. Or Crysse,
who could never be expected to understand what
she'd done in a million years.

There was a stand for the *Chronicle* by the shop
door. A weekend features' box listed her piece about

the holiday cottages for the disadvantaged children and she remembered Emily Wootton's wry invitation to join the volunteers who were going to decorate them.

She stopped. Why not? Why not volunteer, spend a couple of weeks out of sight of everyone she knew while the fuss died down, doing something worthwhile? Something to wear her out so that she didn't lie awake at night wondering where Mike was, what he was thinking.

She'd really rather not know that.

She paid for the paper and the largest, most comforting bar of chocolate to nibble in the event that hard work wasn't enough, and folded the paper back at the feature to look for the number to ring. Holding her purse between her teeth, and with the newspaper and chocolate tucked under her arm, she dug around in the depths of her bag for her phone as she headed in the direction of the restaurant.

Mike saw the queue at the self-service and abruptly changed his mind. He'd buy a can of something cold, and a sandwich from the chill cabinet in the shop to eat in the car. He stepped back, turned and cannoned into someone, sending a cellphone, a newspaper and a big black leather bag flying. For a moment he couldn't move as he was swept by a sickening sensation of *déjà vu*. Then he looked down and was confronted by a pair of electric blue eyes.

Shock treatment.

He waited, his tongue cleaving to the roof of his mouth, expecting Willow to slap him, to let fly with a torrent of abuse that would probably have them both ejected from the building by security staff.

Her mouth opened as she tried to form a word. Then it closed. She swallowed, helplessly. He knew exactly how she felt.

Someone pushed by him, muttering about people blocking the door and he found the use of his limbs, bent to pick up her things. When he straightened she hadn't moved.

'Willow—'

'Mike—'

They both started and both stopped. Then tried again.

'I should have—'

'I didn't mean to—'

Then he said, 'You know, we really must stop meeting like this.'

'Yes.' She blushed this time, and his heart turned over, started beating again. Slowly. Pink and white skin, vivid blue eyes, hair like jet. The effect was not diminished by familiarity. 'I—I was going to get something to eat.'

'The queue is horrendous. I think there must be a coach party.'

'Oh.'

She seemed poised for flight and he put out a hand to stop her. Keep her close. Then he snatched it back before he quite made contact. His memory filled in the blanks, how her skin would feel like silk beneath his fingers, what would follow...

'I don't suppose it will take long to clear,' he said quickly and used his redundant hand to push open the door. To hold it for her. He didn't want her to go anywhere. He had run from the wedding and everything that it symbolised. Not from Willow. 'Shall we risk it?' She hesitated. 'I'd like—'

'An explanation.' Willow wanted to run. Wanted to stay. Wanted to die. To jilt a man at the altar was bad enough. To meet him on the motorway as you made your escape was retribution on a scale dished out by old-time Sunday-school teachers. Be good, or your sins will surely find you out. But he was entitled to an explanation. Not carefully chosen words in a letter, but face to face. It would be harder this way. But afterwards, afterwards she might just feel a bit... She balked at the word, better. Nothing would ever make her feel *better* about what she'd done. 'Yes,' she said.

She took her bag from him, stowed all the stuff she'd been carrying so chaotically about her person, except for the newspaper which wouldn't fit, then walked through the door he was holding for her and took a tray from the pile. Anything to keep her hands occupied. To stop her from throwing herself at him and telling him that she was sorry, that it was all a terrible mistake. That she loved him.

'Are you very hungry?' she asked inanely—she had to say something as they moved along the carefully lit displays of food.

'Not particularly. I just need some coffee and some carbohydrate so that I don't pass out on the motorway. I couldn't face breakfast.'

'Yes. Me too. To both of those...' She glanced at him. 'You didn't, um...' What? Stay? Have lunch with their guests? That would have been fun...

'I thought you'd be at home—'

'With my mother? I can think of more comfortable places to be. Outer Mongolia springs to mind…' Shut up, Willow. Flippancy is not going to help. 'Shall we try the pasta?'

'Anything.' He glanced at the woman waiting to serve them. 'Make that pasta for two.'

Willow picked out a couple of plates of side salad and moved over to the drinks. She flinched from the freshly squeezed orange juice, taking a bottle of mineral water. Mike recoiled from the orange juice, taking a can of cola. 'I'll come back for coffee,' she said, putting the tray down to look for her purse. She couldn't let him pay for her lunch. He paid while she was still searching, his expression suggesting argument was pointless.

'Where are you going?' They'd been pushing the pasta around their plates for a while.

Mike took her question as a cue to give up on the food, and sat back in his chair. 'As far from Melchester as I can before nightfall. I suppose you're on your way to London? The big time?'

'I wasn't thinking about that. I just wanted to get away from my family.'

'The sympathetic looks.'

'I don't know about sympathetic—'

'The sudden embarrassed silence every time you walk into any room, anywhere.' He closed his eyes briefly, as he dwelt on what he'd done to her. 'It was an unforgiveable thing to do.'

'I'm so sorry, Mike—'

'I'm really sorry, Willow—'

They both spoke at the same, the words coming

out one at a time, slow and painful. Then they stopped, looked up.

Willow started again. 'I can't expect you to understand—'

'I can't begin to explain,' Mike said, 'to expect you to—'

Then Willow frowned. 'What are you apologising for, Mike? I'm the one who ran out on the big day. Left you standing at the altar.' She couldn't bear to look at him. 'It was that awful juicer,' she raced on before he could say anything, tell her how much he was hurting. She could see that for herself. He looked grey. 'I had this nightmare picture of me in that vast kitchen, frilly apron, big Stepford-wife smile, every morning for the rest of my life. Squeezing oranges.' He was staring at her. 'I know that's what you wanted, I thought it was what I wanted, but it isn't. Not yet. Not for years—'

'Willow—'

'Actually, I hope I'll never be ready for that.' She sat back. 'Is that a terrible admission? To admit that I want a career more than—?'

'Than me?' he asked.

'It wasn't like that!'

'What was it like?'

She shook her head. How could she explain? 'I realised it as we got to the church. I realised that getting married would be the end of my life, not the beginning, and that was wrong, wasn't it?' He looked bemused, she realised and without thinking reached out, covered his hand with hers. 'I'm so sorry, Mike. I realise now that I pushed you into asking me to marry you. I should never have said yes when you proposed.'

'Why did you? Say yes?'

'Because…because at that moment I *was* sure.' At that moment she'd known she loved him. But she couldn't say that. If she'd loved him, she wouldn't be here. She'd be drinking champagne, she'd be happy…

'And then you were offered a job that made you realise there were more exciting options.'

She would have snatched her hand back, but he'd covered it, holding it between his.

'I'm sorry, Mike. I know that sounds lame, but I don't know what else to say. I wouldn't have hurt you for the world. But don't you see?' she went on, desperate to make him understand. 'Marrying you when I felt like that would have been much worse.' He was looking at her with a rather strange expression and she finally extricated her fingers, embarrassed now at what, just a few hours before, would have been such natural intimacy. 'Was it awful?' she asked. 'Did my mother have hysterics?'

'Probably,' he said, a glint of something almost like humour sparking in his eyes.

'You didn't hang around? I don't blame you. Your parents…they've been so warm, so generous. They'll never understand, will they?'

'Not in a million years.'

'They must hate me.'

'I wouldn't worry about it. You're going to come a very poor second place to me as a target for brickbats.'

'Are you saying they blamed you? But why?'

'I would appear to be an all round disappointment in the son-and-heir stakes.'

'But you didn't do anything, Mike—'

Mike reached out and reclaimed her hand, anything to stop her blaming herself. 'Yes, I did. I don't know whether your mother had hysterics, I have no idea what my father said, I don't know, because I wasn't there.' He realised his fingers were biting into her wrist and let go. '*I* wasn't *there*.'

She frowned. 'I don't understand.'

'I don't expect you to. Nor to forgive me. I don't even know how to begin to explain.' He shook his head. 'It seemed like a lifetime, sitting there, waiting for you to arrive. Thinking.' He stared at the table, trying to get the words right. 'You gave me too much time to think. If you'd been unconventional and arrived as the church clock struck the hour, well maybe we'd be dancing at our reception right now. But the longer I waited, the stronger grew the conviction that I was doing something entirely wrong. Wrong for me, that is. I found myself wondering how I'd feel if you didn't turn up—'

'Relieved,' she said.

His head came up with a jerk that nearly dislocated his neck. 'You, too?'

Startled by his vehemence, she said, 'What?' Her breath was coming in tiny little gasps as what he was saying finally sank in. As she realised what it meant. 'Oh, my lord. You did it, too, didn't you? Bailed out at the last minute.' She felt almost dizzy with relief. 'We both ran out on our wedding.' She felt like laughing, clamped her hand over her mouth to stop herself. Then she said, 'I almost made it to the church,

Mike, but I couldn't do it. Dad asked the driver to go round the block again—'

'Thank God he did. If you'd stopped the first time, I'd probably have still been there.'

'What would you have done?'

'Done?' He looked slightly shell-shocked by her revelation. 'Once you had set foot in the church there wouldn't have been anything to do. Except say ''I will'' and live with the consequences.'

'We came so close…' She tried to hold her finger and thumb a centimetre apart but was shaking too much. Mike caught her hand, held it between his and she looked at him, really looked at him for the first time in weeks and for a moment the words wouldn't come. 'S-so close to making the most almighty mistake,' she said.

'At least our nearest and dearest won't be able to fling blame at each other over lunch. With so much in common, they'll be able to really enjoy themselves. And there'll be no tedious speeches to spoil the fun.'

Willow found herself drawing in a huge breath. It felt like the first real air she'd breathed in days. 'Well. That's all right, then. Isn't it?'

'Is it?'

'You want to go back and face the music?' She found herself grinning at the stir that would cause. Then a ripple of laughter escaped her. 'I don't think so.'

'No.' Then he smiled too. 'What we could do…' She waited. 'We could call Cal and ask him to bring the tickets and our luggage and go to the West Indies anyway.'

She thought about guaranteed sunshine, soft white

beaches and snorkelling in a warm clear sea. She thought about tree frogs chirping into a velvet dark night and Mike making love to her. 'Yes, we could.'

'But?'

'You have to ask?'

'I suppose taking the honeymoon when you've run out on the wedding might raise a few eyebrows.'

Might? 'More than a few.' She let out a long, slow breath. 'We've made a lot of people very unhappy, but they'll understand, might even applaud the fact that we both had the courage to step back from the brink. I don't think that rewarding ourselves with a couple of weeks of total self-indulgence would be viewed with the same tolerance.' Then, with a careless shrug that took more effort that she cared to admit, even to herself. 'It would be a pity to waste the tickets, though. There's no reason why you shouldn't go.'

'On my own?'

'That,' she said, 'is entirely up to you. I'm not in a position to complain if you—'

'No! I meant...' She raised her eyebrows, questioning what exactly he had meant. 'Well, I wasn't thinking of dialling round old girlfriends to see who's free,' he said sharply. Then, raising his hands in a helpless little gesture, he sat back. 'Why don't you go? Take Crysse with you. You're not starting your new job straight away?'

She shook her head. Then, in case he hadn't understood which of those suggestions she was rejecting, 'Not until next month. At least, I've still got to talk to Toby about that. I take it you'll waive the usual notice?' Then, since he didn't seem to think an answer was necessary, she continued, 'And I've just walked out on everything Crysse ever wanted. Asking her along on the abandoned honeymoon trip would be a bit like rubbing salt in her wounds.'

'Sean wasn't inspired by our reckless plunge into matrimony, I take it?'

'No, he wasn't. He found the whole elaborate performance extremely off-putting. Another reason why she won't be totally thrilled with me.'

Mike shrugged. 'Oh, well, I imagine the cancellation insurance covers a no-show at the church.'

'What about a double no-show? Do you get a bonus?' she asked flippantly, anything to stop herself from bursting into tears. Why would she cry when she was so happy? When everything had turned out so well? She might be a runaway bride, but *he* was a runaway groom. So that was all right. Wasn't it? 'Or do you have to pay a penalty?'

He stood up. 'I'll get that coffee.'

'No. Really. I must go.' She got to her feet. Mike stood up, too. Then they both stood there, uncertain how to end it. A kiss seemed inappropriate. Shaking hands, ridiculous.

'I'll look out for your byline in the *Globe*, Willow.' That sounded so final. She didn't want it to be that final. If only she could turn the clock back to that night he'd asked her to move in with him. If she'd just said yes... 'You made the right decision, you know. You should always go for the dream. My mistake was forgetting that.'

'We didn't talk much about our dreams, did we?' she asked sadly. He lifted his shoulders, let them fall in a hopeless gesture that said it all. 'If we hadn't been in such a rush to get married...' What was the point of 'ifs'? What was done, was done. 'Where will you go?'

'Somewhere. Nowhere. Get lost for a few days. You?'

'I'm going to try my hand at the business end of interior design for a change. Help out a friend who needs a hand with some decorating.' A kiss, she realised, would leave her weeping a puddle onto the floor and she stuck out her hand. He took it, but she didn't linger, withdrawing her fingers almost before he'd touched them. 'Goodbye, Mike. Have a nice life.'

She spun round and walked quickly away while she still could. It was too late for regrets. 'Go for the dream,' he'd said and maybe he was right. But it seemed a pity that life could only find room for one dream at a time. She hoped hers was big enough to make up for the hollow ache deep inside her.

Mike watched her walk away and knew that nothing in his life would be as hard again. He wanted to shout her name. Go after her. Tell her how much he wanted her, needed her, loved her still. But then what? He'd suggested to Cal that she had simply been marking time at the *Chronicle* until she got married. He'd been wrong about that. Wrong about so much. She wanted the *Globe*. London. And she'd got it.

As for him, well, he loved her, but not, apparently, with sufficient heat to compromise his own life.

Or maybe he was being hard on himself. Maybe he loved her just enough to realise that in time he would come to resent her for making the compromise necessary. That she would resent him for making her choose.

He slumped back into his seat, giving her time to leave the car park. He couldn't face the awkward little smiles, the nods, as they made their way to their respective vehicles. The silly shrugs of people who have already said goodbye but can't seem to get away from each other. Saying goodbye once had been hard enough.

So he picked up the newspaper that she'd left on the table. It was folded back at a piece about some cottages being renovated to provide holiday accommodation for kids. Kids who had nothing. Which put his problem, that of having too much, into perspective.

Willow switched on her cellphone, ignored the message-waiting icon flashing importantly at her and then realised she hadn't brought the paper with her. She could buy another, but going back would risk walking into Mike again. Walking away three times in one day was never going to be possible.

It hadn't been easy saying no to the honeymoon. It wasn't Mike she'd walked away from. It was the life being his wife would slot her into. She'd begun to realise that before the *Globe's* job offer had dropped on her doorstep. That had been her escape route, not the reason for needing one. She still loved Mike. She always would.

Which was why, instead of going back for a paper, she searched her notebook, flipping back through it until she found Emily's number.

'Willow? I thought you were getting married to-day.'

'There's been a change of plans,' she said with determined brightness. 'It was mutual, but rather public and I need a bolt-hole for a few days. I wondered if you've got a place for an apprentice painter?'

'At the cottages, you mean? You bet. It's a bad time of year to get volunteers. The men are all too busy with gardening or painting their own houses while the sun shines. The women are all too busy nagging them.'

'Well, you've got me—full-time, if you want me. Can I stay there?'

'Well, I suppose so. It isn't furnished, but the water and electricity are all laid on. You just have to throw the switch, turn the stopcock. You'll be on your own at night, though. Will you be all right? Maybe you'd be happier at the village pub. I can give them a call—'

'Thanks, but I'd rather keep a low profile right now.'

'Okay. Well, I'll meet you at the cottages, then. I'll bring a sleeping bag and a few provisions to see you over the weekend.'

Mike stared at the paper but, instead of words, he just kept seeing Willow's arrow-straight back as she'd headed for the door, walking out of his life. And he thought about what he'd said when he'd asked her to marry him. About wanting her there every morning when he woke.

That hadn't changed. Not by a heartbeat. One chance. Two dreams. There had to be a way to make it work and the table rocked as he leapt to his feet and, slamming the door open with the flat of his hand, he raced after her. There was no sign of her little yellow car in the car park and for a moment his heart plummeted. Then a flash of sunlight on a windscreen, just at the corner of his vision, sent him spinning round.

It was Willow. Not heading for London, but going back the way she'd come. Going home after all? Surely not… And suddenly the words that he'd been reading so mindlessly came into focus. Made sense. Decorating. Helping someone, she'd said.

He dashed back into the services and rescued the paper from the woman who was cleaning the table and scanned the page again, this time absorbing every detail. And the details made him smile. It was the perfect opportunity to start over, on the ground floor. And this time he would show her exactly who he was and what he did.

The minute Emily left, Willow set to work. She had nothing else to do. She wasn't hungry and, despite a certain lassitude, the result of reaction to the day's events, she knew she wasn't going to sleep any time soon.

She opened a tin of paint, a glorious shade of sky blue for the day room. A place for the children to play games when the weather was too bad to be outside, a place for them to gather at night for stories and singing. She stirred it with an old wooden spoon provided for the purpose, picked up her paintbrush and began.

She'd been going for about an hour when she heard a car pulling up behind the cottages. Emily had been so worried about leaving her on her own that Willow wasn't particularly surprised, just curious at how inventive she'd be with an excuse for coming back to check on her.

Easing her back, putting down the paintbrush and flexing fingers stiff from being held in one position for so long, stiff with paint, she decided that her visitor wouldn't need an excuse; not if she'd brought a bottle of wine with her. And some fish and chips.

She climbed down from the stepladder, wiped the back of her hand across her cheek and went to open the door. When she saw who was there, she tried to shut it again.

She wasn't quick enough. Mike ducked under the low doorway and was inside while her mouth was still flapping about, having trouble with the 'go away' words the occasion demanded.

Mike, in paint-spattered jeans and a T-shirt that might once have been black, might once have had sleeves. Mike, with a sleeping bag rolled up beneath his arm.

CHAPTER THREE

MIKE dropped the sleeping bag, reached out and rubbed the pad of his thumb over her cheek. It came away sky blue. 'Nice colour, it suits you. But isn't the paint supposed to go on the walls?' His eyes did a quick head-to-toes inspection of her and then he grinned. 'Tell me, sweetheart, have you ever done this before?'

Willow firmly squashed her heart back into place. It had no business to be leaping about in that giddy, unrestrained way. He would have left her at the altar if she hadn't got cold feet on the way to the wedding, she reminded herself. Jilted her. If she hadn't jilted him first. She concentrated on what that would have felt like and resolutely forbade her arms to get their own way and fling themselves about him.

'This is unfair, Mike. What the hell do you think you're doing here?'

'Much the same as you, I guess. At a loose end and feeling the need to do a little good.'

'And you just happened to pick the same place as me?'

'Is that a problem for you?' he asked with a bland expression that she didn't trust. He was up to something. 'Volunteers have been called for. I'm volunteering. I've even brought my own sleeping bag—'

'You can stuff your sleeping bag and your good intentions and find somewhere else to hide out!'

'And a bottle of chilled white wine. I can't guarantee the quality, but the guy in the pub down the road said it was drinkable—'

'I haven't got a corkscrew.'

'And some Chinese food which could probably do with heating up,' he continued as if she hadn't interrupted. 'I thought you might be hungry.'

'Well, I'm not,' she declared roundly. But as the scent of the food reached her from the bag he was carrying, her stomach rebelled, noisily betraying her.

Taking that as a change of heart, he looked around. 'Is the cooker connected?'

'Mike, we made a mistake!' With him there in front of her she knew they'd made a mistake. They'd made a mistake in running away from their problems instead of facing them, but it was too late to change things. And this wasn't helping. 'We both agreed. We said goodbye. Please don't make this any harder...' She stopped. It wasn't *meant* to be hard. She'd *chosen* this.

He appeared not to notice how close she'd been to admitting regret. How close she'd been to giving him her heart on plate. It wasn't her heart he wanted. Not when push came to shove.

'You think I want to be here? This is tough for me, too, sweetheart. But you're going to need some help if this place is going to be ready in time. Volunteers would appear to be a bit thin on the ground.' He headed for the cooker, switched it on and loaded the cartons onto the shelves. When he straightened, he turned and looked at her. 'Just because we decided not to get married, Willow, doesn't mean we can't behave like civilised adults. We can still be friends.'

'Friends!' Outraged, her feelings finally caught up with reality. She didn't want to be *friends*.

'Why not? I like you. I like you a lot.' She looked doubtful. 'What? You surely don't think I kept asking you out just because you're great in bed?' That was a loaded question. She was a loser whatever her answer, so she kept quiet. 'Come on, Willow. We both need to stay out of sight. Let's help one another out, here. For old times sake.'

'We haven't had any *old times*. We've only known one another for a few months.'

'Five months, two weeks, four days. Just because we made the mistake of nearly getting married...' *she wished he wouldn't keep saying that!* '...doesn't mean we have to cross the street to avoid one another. Does it?' He offered her his hand. 'Pax?'

'Pax?' she repeated, keeping her hands to herself, not convinced that it could be that easy. He looked far too innocent to trust. Except she would trust him with her life. 'Friends?'

'*Good* friends, I hope.'

This was the mistake. She was sure of it. The magnetic attraction that had been so fierce, so inescapable from the first moment they met, had not dimmed one jot during those five months, two weeks, four days. But he was right about one thing. What she knew about painting and decorating could be written on a postage stamp. A very small postage stamp.

And the cottages were isolated. It would be good to know there was someone within shouting distance if the floorboards started to creak in the middle of the night.

Her hand slid into his. Warm, strong. For a brief moment, all she'd wanted in the world.

'Just good friends?' That shouldn't have been a question. Her voice ought to have been firmer.

For a brief moment his hand tightened about hers and she was sure his assurance that they would keep things on a platonic basis was just a ruse. Before she could reiterate her determination to keep it that way, though, he released her fingers, turned away to look around at their temporary home and she couldn't be sure whether she was relieved or infuriated that he found it so easy to keep his word.

'It's a bit spartan,' he said, and Willow dragged her thoughts back to reality and thought guiltily of the beautiful kitchen cabinets in their would-be marital home that she'd made such a performance about. 'That wall could do with some shelves.'

'Yes, it could. Do you know a good carpenter?'

'Yes,' he said. Then turned and looked down at her. 'I don't suppose there are any glasses, are there?'

'Disposable cups, that's all.'

'Then, we'll make do with those.' He produced a multi-purpose penknife from his back pocket, opened out the corkscrew and set to work on the bottle of wine. 'Plates?'

'Paper ones.'

'Chopsticks?'

'We'll have to make do with plastic forks.'

He grinned. 'No fighting over the washing up, then.'

'Good friends don't fight, do they?'

'No?' He pulled the cork. 'Maybe not. But then, we never did fight.' He filled two of the plastic cups she produced from a cupboard. 'We always had better things to do.' Willow turned swiftly away, checked the food. 'How is it?'

Painful. She'd been such an idiot. They could have been in Mike's flat right now. Or hers. Curled up together with nothing better to do than be together. If she'd just stayed put that Sunday night, for once indulged the man she loved. But no, that would have been breaking her own rules.

She'd thought she was so damned smart. But she wasn't smart. She was arrogant and stupid and now she was paying the price. Now and for ever.

Mike had obviously never really wanted marriage or he wouldn't have beaten a hasty retreat from the church. He'd just been carried away by the heat of his libido.

But what was her excuse? Hot grey eyes that promised her the earth? And delivered...

'Another few minutes to be on the safe side, I think.' She fixed a smile to her lips, then turned and took the cup of wine he offered, spilling a few drops as his fingers brushed against hers. 'So, what's the toast, Mike?' she asked brightly. 'The great escape?'

For a moment the muscles in his jaw tightened, then he too managed a smile. 'Sure, why not?' But he took little more than a sip of the wine before putting the cup down on the draining-board. 'Why don't you show me round while we're waiting.'

'There's not much to see.' The holiday centre had been converted from a row of artisans' cottages and the rooms all opened from a single corridor, with a staircase at each end.

'Downstairs there's the kitchen, dining room, day

room, quiet room.' She led the way, opening doors without stopping, taking the stairs swiftly to keep a pace ahead of him, so she wouldn't feel his breath on her neck. 'And upstairs, two big rooms that'll have bunk beds for the kids,' she said breathlessly. 'Showers and wash basins. Girls here. Boys there. Toilet facilities. Two small bedrooms for the carers.'

He pushed open doors and looked in as she whisked past. Noted her sleeping bag laid out in one of the small rooms. The bag she'd packed before taking to the hills. It looked lonely all by itself. The second small room looked even lonelier.

'It's a heck of a lot for one woman to paint.'

'It's not just me. There'll be other people. I'll bet Emily's phone has been ringing off the hook all day,' she said defiantly. 'Please don't think you have to stay.'

'I don't. I don't have to do anything. I'll stay because I want to.'

Mike looked down into the face of the one woman he'd ever wanted to keep so close to him that it hurt. To win her, keep her, he'd compromised his life, pretended that he was someone he could never be. And somehow she'd known. Not in her head, maybe, but in her heart where it mattered, she'd known that something was wrong.

This time he would do it right. If she was going to walk away from him, she'd walk away from the man he was, not the man he'd tried to be.

'I promise you, Willow, from this day on I will live my life on my own terms.' And just for a moment he thought that a quiver of desperation blurred the fierce determination of her face, giving him heart. 'No more fudging, no more compromise.'

Willow's grip tightened on the door handle. 'Was that how our relationship was for you?' she asked, her face betraying a world of hurt. 'A fudge? A compromise?' He reached out, wanting to reassure her that he hadn't meant it that way. 'The truth, Mike.'

The truth. He wanted to tell her that the relationship was the one thing that had been true. But that wasn't what she was asking. 'Yes,' he admitted. 'I was compromising, doing stuff I didn't want to do. You?'

'Yes, of course I was.' Then, because if they stayed where they were another second she'd probably burst into tears, she said, 'The food will be thoroughly reheated by now.' And she turned and half stumbled down the stairs in her haste to put some space between them.

'This is excellent.' Willow, sitting cross-legged on the cottage's floor, speared a prawn. 'Where did it come from?'

'Maybridge. There's a little place down by the lock where the food is quite special.'

She glanced up. Maybridge? What had he been doing in Maybridge? Going back? Picking up the threads of the life he'd had before his father's ill health had brought him home?

'It's pretty there, along by the river,' she said.

'I always meant to take you...' He shrugged. 'Still, you'll have the whole of London to choose from when you're working on the *Globe*.'

She didn't care about London. She wanted to know about Maybridge. 'You worked there...' she couldn't stop herself '...before your father was taken ill?' He looked at her as if assessing where her question was leading. Then he nodded. 'You've never talked about it.' It wasn't that she hadn't been interested in his life before she'd known him. It was just that her curiosity had encountered an invisible barrier. He'd turned the conversation away from the past, distracted her. He was good at that. 'You quarrelled with your father, didn't you?'

'Was that what the office gossips told you?'

It was her turn to nod. 'Yes.'

'I didn't quarrel with him, Willow. It's just that I'm not excited by balance sheets, cash flow, advertising revenue. I needed something else. My father couldn't understand that, so it was easier if I stayed away.'

'Did you find what you were looking for, Mike? In Maybridge.'

'Some of it.' He looked up then. 'Then I came home and found the rest.'

His eyes assured her that she was everything he'd been missing. But it hadn't been enough. It scared her that she could have been so inattentive, so self-absorbed in her own problems these past few weeks that she'd been oblivious to whatever had been eating away at him, bringing him to the point of flight.

Mike, sitting with his back against the wall, one knee drawn up to balance his plate, returned his attention to his food. 'You never talk about yourself, do you?' she persisted.

'It's a most unattractive habit.'

She was on a fishing expedition, he realised; dangling supposition in the hope that he would give her the reality. He'd not been very forthcoming about what he'd been doing for the past few years but, then, she hadn't been very pressing.

No, that wasn't fair. She been interested, he'd been the one who'd always changed the subject, uncertain of her reaction. Self-preservation had kept his mouth shut, even when he'd wanted to pour out his heart and soul.

He lifted one brow, to let her know that he was on to her. 'Is that it? End of interrogation?'

'Yes,' she said. And her acceptance, reluctant though it was, left him oddly disappointed. He wanted her to *demand* answers, *insist* on them. But why would she? She had another life all planned out. One that didn't include him.

No, Willow thought, chasing a prawn about the plate. He'd told her nothing. But maybe it was too late to fill in the gaps. They should have been doing that weeks ago, except that when they were together he hadn't wanted to tell her.

Now they were apart she was damned if she was going to betray her regrets by asking questions he had no intention of answering.

'I am sorry, Mike...' she made one of those help-less little gestures that she so loathed in other people '...about messing up your takeover of the company. Will your father still be prepared to go ahead and transfer the paper to you?'

'I'm afraid so. Armstrong Publications is more im-portant than a little public embarrassment. He'll need a week or two to convince himself that you were to blame for what happened today before he'll admit it, but it shouldn't take longer than that. He's good at deluding himself.'

'Don't be cruel! He loves you.' Then she said, 'A week or two? That's all it'll take?'

'He has an infinite capacity for self-deception.' Maybe it was hereditary. He'd followed Willow in the belief that it was possible to win her back. He wasn't doing much of a job, probably because he understood so well what was driving her. All his life people had wanted him to do what they wanted. He wouldn't, couldn't do that to her. If she really wanted London, the *Globe*, then she must have it. He wanted his life in Maybridge. Somehow he had to find a way to fit them into a life they could share. 'Do you want some more of this, or shall I finish it?'

About to apologise again, try and make him see why she hadn't been able to go through with the wedding, Willow stopped herself. He was as much to blame as she was for his fall from grace. He'd asked her to marry him. She hadn't twisted his arm. Her only mistake had been to say yes. Everyone knew you shouldn't say yes straight away—not that it would have made any difference. If she'd thought about it for a second or a year, her answer would still have been the same.

'Willow?'

'What? Oh, no, go ahead. Finish it all. I wasn't as hungry as I thought. In fact, I think I'll take a shower and then try and get some sleep.'

'Will you be all right up there on your own?'

Mistrusting the concerned note in his voice, still sure that he was would try and move the 'just good friends' goal posts a little—this was the jilting man, after all, who'd suggested they could still go on honeymoon—she rounded on him, determined to put him right about that. But he looked so serious that she stopped pushing the food trays back into the carrier bag.

'Why shouldn't I be?'

'No reason.' Then he added, 'Just give a shout if you need me to evict that spider from the shower room.'

She swallowed. 'Spider?'

'A big black one with hairy legs. I noticed it in the girls' showers when we did that whistle-stop tour.'

'Then I'll use the boys'.'

'Willow—'

'And your room is the one at the far end.' Just in case he had any lingering hope that she might be prepared to share hers.

'Willow—'

'What?'

'Nothing, sweetheart.' His slow smile was an essay in the art of teasing. 'I'll lock up.'

She swept up the stairs—or she would have if she hadn't been wearing jeans and a T-shirt stiff with paint—convinced she could hear him laughing. Let him laugh, she was damned if she would yell for help. She could cope with a spider. If she had to.

But she bypassed the girls' shower room and when cautious inspection revealed that the boys' was a spider-free zone, she turned on the water in the first stall, adjusting the temperature. She'd stripped down to her underwear when she realised she had a bigger problem than spiders.

No soap. And no towel.

She'd thrown a change of clothes into her bag

thinking… No, that was an exaggeration. She hadn't been thinking. She hadn't been thinking for weeks.

She fetched a clean T-shirt from her bag and pulled it over her bra, then went to the top of the stairs. 'Mike!' His face appeared below her. 'Could you throw up that bar of soap on the kitchen sink.'

He didn't throw it, he brought it up. 'It's a bit basic,' he said, sniffing at it.

'Basic is fine. I need something capable of shifting paint.' Then she asked, 'I don't suppose you thought to bring a towel with you, did you?'

'Sorry, I'm a man on the run. I didn't get beyond a razor and a change of clothes. To be honest, I envisaged staying in an hotel tonight.'

'You could try the pub. They do rooms.'

'Sounds inviting. What about you?'

'I'm happy where I am…'

'In that case I'll dry myself with a spare T-shirt.' He grinned. 'You can share if you like.'

'Thanks, but I've got my own.'

'Mine's bigger.'

'Don't brag, Mike.' She took the soap from him. Then she demanded, 'What are you doing?' as he peeled off his T-shirt, unhooked his belt. He dropped his trousers, kicked them off and stepped into the end stall, so that only his head and shoulders were visible. 'Mike, you can't do this!'

His boxers joined the rest of his clothes on the floor. 'When you use the boys' room, honey, you have to be prepared to share.' And he turned on the water. 'Take your pick. Spiders or me.'

She knew she was being silly. What difference did

a day make? A hell of a lot. 'Mike, this is impossible. You jilted me.'

'The words "pot" and "kettle" spring to mind, but I'm not whining. Nobody says you have to look.'

'I'm not looking!' She stamped but, shoeless, she might as well not have bothered.

'Pass the soap, will you?' He extended his hand and she passed it to him. 'And next time you stamp your foot, watch that beetle. He hasn't done anything to you.'

'Beetle? You expect me to fall for that?' Then something with scratchy legs ran over her foot and she screamed and leapt in the shower stall with him. 'Where did that come from?'

'In here,' he said, grinning broadly as she stepped back. Except with his body blocking the exit, there wasn't anywhere to go.

'You rat!'

'Nobody's perfect.' He reached up to soap his hair, his arm brushing against her, doing nothing for her determination to keep this platonic.

'Excuse me,' she said, attempting to extricate herself without touching any more of him than was absolutely necessary. 'These aren't exactly made for two.'

His arm was around her waist in a heartbeat. 'That beetle is lying in wait for you.'

'Please, Mike…'

His eyes darkened. 'You should get out of those wet things, you know. You'll catch cold.'

She swallowed, but found it impossible to look away, pull free, although his arm was loose about her waist, his hold anything but imprisoning. 'This relationship is over.' She made her mouth say the words, but she knew that her body, responding mindlessly to his touch, was giving him an entirely different message.

'Is it?' he asked softly. Then, not waiting for an answer, his mouth came down on hers, tender, undemanding, still offering her the choice to say no. Irresistible. For a moment she didn't resist. Just for a moment, with the warm water pouring over her, soaking into her T-shirt, into her underwear, she let herself drown in the honey of his mouth, let herself be drawn into the sweet deception that this was a relationship still going somewhere. Then she caught his wet shoulders with her hands and pushed herself away from him. He made no attempt to stop her, there was nowhere for her to go. He just said, 'Over?'

'It has to be. I want a career. I don't know what you want.'

'You,' he said.

She didn't doubt it. She knew that look. She swallowed nervously. 'So how come we were having pasta on the motorway when we should have been knee-deep in smoked salmon and champagne?' She banged her elbow on the taps and seized the chance to say something very rude to cover the hurt she was feeling.

'You're right. These shower stalls were definitely built with single occupancy in mind,' Mike said as he ran his fingers gently along her arm, checking for damage.

'It's basic,' Willow agreed. 'But at least it hasn't got those disgusting gold taps.' And for a moment they shared a vision of the huge shower stall in the house they should have been moving into.

'That's a bonus,' he agreed after a moment. Then, glancing at her, he said, 'I thought you liked them. You waxed positively lyrical when Dad gave us the grand tour of the house.'

'He'd just given it to us as a wedding present. What did you expect me to say?'

He stilled. 'You really didn't like the taps?'

She shrugged. 'They were rather…ornate, for my taste. You?'

'I prefer things to be simple and functional,' he agreed.

'Then, this should suit you fine. But if you've finished, I'd be grateful if you'd get out and let me take a shower—*alone*—in peace.'

By the time she'd finished, he'd dried himself with his T-shirt and was respectably clad in trousers. She mopped herself dry as best she could and then felt positively naked in a pair of knickers and a damp T-shirt that clung to her breasts. She shivered. 'It's cold now, isn't it?'

'Not from where I'm standing.'

They parted at her bedroom door. 'I'll see you in the morning,' Willow said awkwardly, as he turned to go. It seemed entirely wrong to sleep in separate rooms, to be apart. It would have been so comforting to have his arms around her tonight, some reassurance that she hadn't stepped off the edge of the world without a parachute.

'Not before nine-thirty on a Sunday,' he warned. 'And I take three spoonfuls of sugar in my tea.' He almost smiled as he bent and lightly brushed her cheek with his lips. 'But you already know that.'

She shut the door in his face. But only to stop herself from hooking her fingers into his waistband and dragging him inside with her.

Willow had always assumed that the country was quiet. There was no traffic hum to disturb her, it was true, but the house was full of noises as the air cooled and the old timbers creaked and settled. Above her in the attic space, small creatures shifted and rustled. Mice. Or bats.

But it wasn't the thought of bats, zipping in under the eaves with the smug, sitting-tenant assurance of a protected species, that was keeping her awake.

Her body might ache from her efforts with a paintbrush, but her mind simply refused to shut down, instead constantly rerunning in slow motion the low points of her day.

What a mess.

She reached for her mobile, switched it on. The message-waiting icon still flashed urgently. Her mother, as she'd anticipated, every hour on the hour, demanding that she ring. Her father, just asking that she let them know she was safe. She should have done that hours ago. Crysse, almost incoherent in her inability to comprehend what she'd done.

Willow hadn't thought it possible to feel any worse. Which showed how much she knew. She tried to return Crysse's call, but the phone just rang and rang. Even the answering machine refused to listen to her excuses.

Her father, though, answered on the first ring, as if

he'd been sitting by the phone, waiting to snatch it off the hook. He didn't ask where she was, only how she was coping.

'I'm fine, Dad. Really. I'm at Marlowe Court, help-ing put the finishing touches to the holiday cottages I was telling you about. I just need to be alone for a while.' And to do something for somebody else after weeks of what, in retrospect, appeared to have been mindless selfishness.

'Is there anything you need? Anything I can bring you?'

A dozen things sprang immediately into her mind, but she'd manage without them. Not even her father would understand about Mike being here. She didn't understand it herself. Especially the fact that she was glad he was curled up in his sleeping bag in the room at the other end of the corridor. Near enough if she called out… 'No. I'll manage. And I'd rather you didn't tell Mum—'

'I won't.' Then he said, 'Willow, about Mike—'

'Dad—'

'Well, don't worry about him, okay? He took it like a man.'

'But Dad—'

'Your mother's coming. Unless you're ready for a lecture, I suggest you hang up now.'

She bit her lip as tears welled up beneath her lids. The sweet man wasn't going to tell her that Mike had run out on her. Despite the dreadful day that she had put him through, her father still wanted to save her feelings. But it didn't make her feel better. She felt infinitely worse. Only one person could do anything to help but he was at the far end of the corridor. She looked around, hoping for a lurking spider to give her an excuse to go running down there and put her sleeping bag next to his.

That was the trouble with spiders. There was never one about when you needed one.

She took a deep breath. She didn't need one. She was fine. She had a life to plan—one that didn't include Mike. She sniffed, searched for a tissue and blew her nose. She didn't have time to mope.

Mike heard the urgent shrill of Willow's phone as she turned it on, alerting her to messages waiting. She'd be calling Crysse. Or her mother. Neither of them calls to look forward to. He should have thought of some way to get her in here with him. She shouldn't be on her own in the dark in a strange place.

Well, maybe it wasn't too late.

He found his mobile and sent her a text message.

Willow's phone beeped again. A text message this time. Crysse?

'Are you okay down there?'

Not Crysse. Mike.

'Absolutely fine,' she tapped in and despatched to him.

Another beep. *'No spiders, beetles or earwigs?'*

Earwigs? Eeugh! That was a low blow. He knew she hated creepy crawlies and he also knew she was lying on the floor in the dark, tucked into the sleeping bag, with only the light of her phone for company. It was too easy to believe that any loose strand of cotton brushing against her ankle was something far worse.

She bit down on her lip, telling herself not to be a wimp.

'Only bats. Any ideas?'

'Close the window?'

'I'd rather risk the bats. Goodnight.'

Mike grinned. *'Did you hear something on the stairs? Is this place haunted?'* he asked.

Willow wished she hadn't bothered to look at that one. After the heat of the day the building creaked and sighed like a restless ghost and it wouldn't stretch her imagination to convince herself that those were footsteps on the stairs.

The phone beeped again. She tried to ignore it, but couldn't. The message read, *'Scream if you need me.'*

Very funny. There was nothing here to bother her except the man at the end of the corridor.

On the other hand, why suffer alone?

She screamed.

He was in the open doorway in a heartbeat, moonlit temptation in soft grey boxers and a frown. 'What is it? What's wrong?'

For a moment she considered telling him that there was something crawling about at the bottom of her sleeping bag. That he'd have to get in there and have a good look around. Then reality kicked in.

'Just testing,' she said.

For a moment he remained where he was. Then he said, 'The system worked.'

'Terrific.'

'Yeah. Goodnight.'

'Night,' she said with a smile that hurt and a little wiggle of her fingers that were all she was prepared to allow out of the sleeping bag. Until he shut the door. Then she dived for her bag, looking for the slab of chocolate she'd bought anticipating low moments. This was definitely a chocolate moment.

'Tea, three sugars.'

Mike's hand appeared from the humped-up sleeping bag followed by a groan as he blearily checked the time on his wrist-watch. 'It's six-thirty, woman. You're inhuman.'

'No one said you had to volunteer.' Life, Willow thought, would be a whole lot simpler if he'd go away. Bleaker, but simpler. 'But the sun's shining and I've got a room to paint.' She put the plastic cup on the floor beside him.

'I don't get breakfast?'

'If you'd wanted room service you should have stayed at the pub,' she said briskly.

'I can't work all day on a cup of tea.' He sat up, raked his hand through his hair, pushing it out of his eyes, and reached for the cup. 'A couple of eggs. Is that too much to ask?'

'Not at all. You'll find a box in the fridge. And Emily thoughtfully brought along a frying pan.'

'What about you?' Mike regarded her with a look that might, by someone inclined to self-deception, be interpreted as concern. 'I'm in enough trouble without you passing out at the top of a stepladder. Breakfast is the most—'

'—important meal of the day. I know.' She tried to look irritated, but it was difficult. He had the kind of shoulders that, naked, bypassed her irritation and went straight for the midriff. Her decision not to marry the man had done absolutely nothing to lessen his physical attraction. 'Tell the truth, Mike. My mother sent you, didn't she?'

Invoking the spectre of her mother should have been sufficient to break the spell. Unfortunately, his grin had a way of making her go weak at the knees. 'I can see there's no point in talking to you. You paint, I'll cook.' He made a move and she beat a hasty retreat before he shucked off the sleeping bag. The grey boxers were on top of a pile of clothes and a man who hadn't stopped to pack a towel wouldn't have given pyjamas a second thought.

She frowned. And what kind of hotel asked you to bring your own sleeping bag?

Halfway down the stairs, she stopped, glanced back. He must have seen the paper at the service station, worked out where she was going. Not so difficult. But that sleeping bag was a long way from new. Where had it come from?

Maybridge. That's where. Did he have stuff stored there? Did he still have a flat or house there? What was it about Maybridge that was so *secret*?

She picked up her tea, walked through to the day room. She'd abandoned her work when Mike had arrived, and expected to find her paintbrush stiff and in need of washing. Instead, it was sitting beside the paint tin, clean, soft and ready to use. She flipped the bristles across the palm of her hand and smiled.

'You'll have to do that yourself from now on.' She looked back over her shoulder at Mike in just his jeans leaning against the doorway, cup in hand, watching her. He really should wear more clothes, she thought. But maybe his T-shirt was still damp from double duty as a towel the night before. She'd hung hers over the window catch to dry, along with the underwear she'd rinsed out in the middle of the night when the chocolate high had suddenly dropped to sea level.

'Thanks for taking care of it. I won't be such a paintbrush slob again.' He didn't seem in any hurry to move. 'What are you going to do?'

'Make myself a fried egg sandwich. Sure I can't interest you?'

'Absolutely certain. I meant where are you going to start painting?'

'I'm not, I'm going to a D-I-Y store. Want to come?'

She just about managed to stop her jaw from dropping. 'Be seen in public with you after yesterday?' she asked, once she'd got her breath back. 'Risk meeting someone I know? Wouldn't that make a tasty morsel for the *Evening Post*'s gossip column.'

'You have a point, but I'm not going to the one on the bypass, I'm going to one at the business park.'

'Near Maybridge?' The words were out before she could stop them.

He grinned. 'That's the one. Are you *sure* you don't want to come?' His voice teased, as if he knew that her curiosity was straining wildly at the leash. 'We could take a walk by the river. Feed the ducks,' he offered, temptingly. 'Have lunch somewhere quiet.'

'Quite sure,' she snapped primly, carefully dipping the brush in the paint, wiping off the excess against the side of the tin and then applying it to the wall. Then curiosity got the better of her. 'What are you going to a do-itself-yourself place for? We've got all the paint and brushes and stuff we need to finish this job.'

'I'm going to get some timber. I thought I'd make a start on some shelves for the kitchen.'

'You?'

'Me.'

'Don't you think you should ask Emily before you do that?'

'Emily?'

'She's the Trust's co-ordinator. I'd assumed you'd read my article in the *Chronicle*. Isn't that how you worked out where I was?'

'I assumed you left it behind so that I would.' She snorted, outraged. 'You don't have to worry, I wasn't planning on charging her for them.'

'That's not what I meant. I meant—'

'You meant, do I know a hammer from a chisel?'

'Well, do you?'

'Just because you've never seen me use anything more dangerous than a fountain pen, Willow, doesn't mean I don't know how.'

'There's an awful lot about you I don't know— considering I was going to marry you.' For instance: she knew why she'd jilted him, but why had *he* jilted *her*? 'What were you thinking about while you were waiting, Mike? In church?'

CHAPTER FOUR

'WILLOW—'

'No,' she said quickly, holding up her hand. 'Forget I asked. Please.' There were some questions that shouldn't be asked.

For a moment she thought he was going to tell her anyway. Then, with a shrug, he let it go. 'What colour is the kitchen going to be?'

'White,' she snapped, irritated by the ease with which he changed the subject. Just because a question shouldn't be asked, didn't mean she didn't really want to *know*!

'Red paint for the shelves, then? Or yellow? Or is that a bit obvious?'

'Purple, green, sky-blue, pink with orange dots. They're your shelves, you decide.'

He tutted, tormentingly. 'There's no need to get in a snit just because your blood-sugar level is low. Sure I can't tempt you to some breakfast before I measure up?'

'Quite sure.'

Her stomach grumbled pitifully as the smell of eggs frying reached her, but she stayed where she was, covering the wall and herself with blue silk emulsion.

She'd almost finished one side of the room before Mike interrupted her again. 'Okay, you've made your point. Now take a break, have some coffee.' She straightened, eased her back and took the cup from him. 'Chocolate biscuit?'

'You know all my weaknesses.'

'Intimately,' he agreed as she took a biscuit from the packet he offered.

Her gaze collided with his. 'Memo to brain, ' she murmured. 'Engage thought processes before opening mouth.'

'Don't do that. Never do that. Always say what's in your heart...' Then he, too, seemed to think twice and the words faltered, stopped. 'I'm going now. You'll be all right here on your own?'

'For heaven's sake—' she began irritably. Then she shrugged. 'Anyone would think I wasn't fit to be allowed out unaccompanied.'

Mike grinned and the dangerous moment passed. 'I refuse to comment on the grounds that I might incriminate myself. See you later.'

'Mike!' He turned back. 'You'd better take a key. I'm going to drive down into the village and see if I can get a few things from the 8 'til Late. Shampoo and stuff. They might even have some towels.' For a moment Willow stood there, thinking about the pile of fluffy white towels that a great aunt had sent them for a wedding present. They were at her flat, along with all the rest of their presents, waiting for the new house to be ready so that they could move in. They'd all have to be returned with some attempt at an explanation. A job she couldn't ask anyone else to do for her. 'There's a spare in the kitchen drawer.' Then she said, 'Do you need anything?'

'I refer to the answer I gave earlier,' he said. By the time she'd mentally backtracked through their conversation and settled on his refusal to answer on the grounds of self-incrimination, his four-by-four was disappearing in the direction of the main road.

Hinton Marlowe boasted a small general store and Willow browsed along the shelves of the shop, searching out the essentials she'd forgotten. Most of them, in fact, except a toothbrush and toothpaste, which were part of her handbag kit. Body wash and shampoo, definitely. Hand cream, absolutely. Rubber gloves seemed like a good idea. Could you paint in rubber gloves? She turned to a man stocking the shelves.

'I don't suppose you sell towels, do you?'

He looked up, then straightened, smiled. 'I think there are some tea towels over there by the washing-up liquid,' he said in a brown-velvet voice. As she followed him across the shop it was impossible to ignore the way his jeans clung to his backside. 'Will they do?' She'd bet he was on the shopping list of every woman in a thirty-mile radius of the village.

She realised he was waiting for an answer. 'Oh.' The tea towels were small, but thick. Better than nothing. 'Yes, thanks.' She browsed for a while, filling her basket with a supply of basic foods to keep them going for a few days, then crossed to the counter. The shelf stocker followed her to take her money.

'Have you just moved into the village?' he asked as he rang up her purchases.

She found her wallet and looked up. 'No. What makes you think that?'

'You're decorating.'

It wasn't a question. She looked down at her T-shirt, but she'd changed it before she came out. 'It's your hair,' he said. 'It's spattered with blue paint.' He grinned with the easy confidence of a man who knows he doesn't have to try too hard. 'It looks good on you though.'

'Thanks—I think,' she said, trying not to remember that Mike had said much the same thing when he'd wiped the stuff off her cheek with his thumb. She really needed not to think about the way he touched her, the way it made her feel cherished, loved.

'So? Will Aunt Lucy be having the pleasure of your custom?' She must have looked blank because he said, 'Use it or lose it. The village store is the centre of the community and Aunt Lucy runs this one.'

'Oh, right. Yes. Or rather, no.'

The grin deepened. 'Are you always this decisive?'

Oh, please! Flirting, she could do without. 'I don't live here, I'm helping out at the Trust cottages at Marlowe Park. Decorating.'

'I heard they were looking for volunteers. Maybe I'll come along and give you a hand.'

'I wouldn't have thought you had a lot of time,' she said, not wanting to sound discouraging—they needed the help—but definitely not wanting to sound as if she was panting for his company.

'With the shop you mean? I'm just helping Aunt Lucy out for a couple of days, carrying boxes, filling shelves during the day.' A slight pause invited her to ask what he did with his evenings. She ignored it. 'The lad who usually does it is on holiday. Would a part-timer be welcome at the cottages?'

'Many hands make light work,' she assured him.

'Give Emily Wootton a ring if you want to volunteer,' she advised, distancing herself from whatever decision he made. 'I've got her number here somewhere.' She found her notebook and wrote Emily's number on a discarded till receipt.

'Thanks…' His eyebrows invited her to fill in the gap with her name.

'Willow,' she said. 'Willow Blake.'

'Thanks, Willow.' He offered her his hand. 'Jacob Hallam.'

'Jacob,' she acknowledged, taking his hand for the briefest moment. Then she paid for her shopping and beat a hasty retreat before he suggested closing the shop and adjourning to the pub to discuss his painting technique.

She returned to the holiday cottages by turns dawdling, scarcely able to bear the thought of seeing Mike again, to see him but not to be able to reach out, touch him, hold him, be part of him. And then foot down, unable to wait another moment…

As she swung around into the parking space behind the cottages, heart hammering, there was only Emily's battered van to keep her car company. She felt like a balloon with the air let out. Flat and joyless.

Emily looked up as Willow joined her upstairs where she was making a start on one of the bedrooms. 'I understand you've got company.' She dipped her brush into the paint and carried on. 'Mike phoned me this morning.'

'Oh?'

'Are you okay with him being here? I'll tell him to get lost if you'd like me to.'

'No, I can handle it.'

'That's a relief. He's offered to make some shelves and we can certainly do with them.'

'I hope he knows what he's doing.' The idea of Mike with a saw in his hands, making shelves, was an entirely new concept, but she'd be lying if she said the prospect of seeing him stripped to the waist and working up a sweat wasn't thoroughly appealing. 'I might have got a new recruit. Jacob Hallam. He's helping out in the village shop. I gave him your number.'

'Oh, right.' Emily grinned broadly. 'Now I see my mistake. I shouldn't have asked for volunteers to help out of the goodness of their hearts, I should have put a big picture of you in the paper and said, come and have some fun with Willow Blake. I'd have been fighting them off.' Then, perhaps remembering that her number one volunteer shouldn't have been available as an attraction for lustful men with a talent for decorating, she rapidly changed the subject. 'I brought some sandwiches. They're in the fridge, if you're hungry.'

Willow forced a sandwich down before setting to work, constantly on the listen for Mike. Then, when he finally did turn up, she just kept going, refusing to rush out so that he'd see just how much she'd missed him. And he didn't come rushing in to see her, either. She heard him talking to Emily and, later, the sound of an electric handsaw being applied to wood.

She tried to ignore it, but after a while—only because she had to stand up and move anyway—she glanced out of the window, watched him for a little while, measuring, marking, cutting.

He did it with the same ease and familiarity with

which he approached an auditor's report. Not happier exactly, but relaxed, in his element with his corn-silk hair powdered with fine sawdust, sawdust streaked across his finely muscled torso. She wanted to put out her hand to see how it felt beneath her fingers.

He could still do it to her, would still be able to do it when she was ninety. That odd breathless catch at her throat, the stirring of the fine hairs at her nape, an atavistic yearning for one man, her man, linked her with all women, back through to the distant ages.

But they had more than that. Their relationship had matured, deepened beyond the driving physical urge to mate, procreate, that brought men and women to-gether.

She longed to cherish Mike, to care for him, grow old with him, wherever life might take them. So how, with all that, could they have been so careless with what they'd been given?

She watched him for a long time but he didn't once look her way.

Maybe that was why she didn't react when, a while later, she heard him come into the day room. She was down on the floor, working close to the skirting board. Getting up was going to be painful and she wasn't doing it until she'd finished.

He didn't speak and she jumped as he put his hands on her shoulders, then gradually relaxed as he began to knead at the ache between her shoulder blades with his thumbs. It was blissful. He seemed to know ex-actly where her muscles were screaming for relief and it felt so good that she didn't want him to stop. Ever.

Then, as his hands moved across her shoulders,

feathering over the sensitive nerve endings that he knew reduced her to jelly, it felt a whole lot better.

Not fair. Not fair.

'Where have you been all day?' Willow demanded, pulling away while she still could. 'It doesn't take this long to buy a couple of planks of wood.'

'You missed me?'

'Like I missed you at the altar,' she retorted.

'Yeah. Right.' He sat back on his heels. 'You know, this isn't an endurance test, Willow,' he said softly. 'Leave it now. Come and have something to eat.'

'I'll eat when I'm good and ready.'

He didn't argue with her, but stood up. 'Better make it soon. You're getting cranky.' She glared at him and he held up his hands, palms out, as if to fend off her wrath. 'Okay, okay, it was just a suggestion.'

She watched him walk away. She stood up, balanced the paintbrush across the tin and peeled off the rubber gloves. She wasn't having him saying she was cranky. Why would she be cranky? She had reclaimed her life, got exactly what she wanted.

She followed him into the kitchen, picked up the kettle and began to fill it. 'Where's Emily?'

'She had to go. She said to tell you goodbye and that she'll try and get over tomorrow afternoon.' Then he asked, 'Do you fancy a bar meal at the pub tonight?'

'Looking like this?'

Mike refrained from telling her that he'd never seen her looking more desirable. She'd almost certainly hit him with the kettle if he did and he'd probably deserve it.

'Honestly, hon, I'm sure once people have seen the blue-speckled look they'll all want it—' He stepped back sharply as she splashed cold water at him, holding up his hands in a gesture of surrender. 'It's the pub or sandwiches again. You choose. But I warn you, cooking utensils seem to be limited to a frying pan.' And besides, he didn't think staying in was such a great idea. What would they do? Uh-huh. Belay that thought. He'd given himself a good talking to about sharing showers, about hands-on muscle-relaxing therapy. 'It's a warm evening,' he added quickly, before his good intentions took a hike. 'We can sit outside.'

'You certainly know how to give a girl a good time.'

'I was the one who suggested St Lucia, remember? You were the one who thought this would be more fun.' He crossed to the sink, standing behind her, his hands hovering an inch from her shoulders, desperate for her warmth. There was no excuse here. No pretence that he was simply easing her shoulders. Besides, he'd blown that one when his fingers got ambitious. 'You don't have to punish yourself, sweetheart,' he said gently. 'You haven't done anything bad.'

She looked back and up at him. 'I don't suppose you could get that in writing from my mother, could you?'

'She wasn't the only one who got it wrong, you know.'

'I know. I should have been tougher about the bridesmaids.' She plugged in the kettle. 'And the cake. No one needs a cake that big. What do you suppose will happen to it?'

He hadn't been thinking about the wedding arrangements. He'd been thinking about his father and that wretched house. But that was his nightmare, not hers. Well, maybe they'd agreed on the hideousness of the taps... 'I'm sure the caterers will find a good home for it.'

'But it had our names and the date inscribed in icing...' She stopped. 'I'm just being silly, aren't I? They'll have them scraped off and something else in their place in ten minutes flat.' Willow took a deep breath. 'That's good. I hate waste—' She turned and he was still there and she laid her cheek against his chest and his arms went around her, holding her. It didn't mean anything. It was just a cuddle. Friends did that, didn't they? Cuddled you when you were down?

He kept telling himself it didn't mean anything. It was just reaction. She was upset. But he loved her, wanted her. If he could be transported back to the church...

Talk about fooling himself. She hadn't come to the church. He could have waited for her until he turned to dust and she would never have turned up. She didn't want him when he was Michael Armstrong, heir apparent to Armstrong Publications, a thriving company in a vibrant city. Why would she want him as Mike Armstrong, head of nothing more important than a little workshop that might have a customer-waiting list two years' long, but would never turn out more than one or two pieces of furniture a month?

He didn't try to hold her as she pulled away, rubbing the back of her hand across her cheek in an attempt to wipe away the tears. 'I'll make that tea.' She sniffed. Mike tore a couple of sheets of kitchen paper from a roll on the draining board and lifting her chin, blotted her cheeks dry. 'It's the smell of the paint,' she said. 'It's making my eyes run.'

He didn't contradict her. 'You need some fresh air, I expect. We could walk across the fields to the village.'

'Give me a couple of hours to scrape off the paint.' Willow sniffed again, then made herself turn away from the broad wall of his chest, the temptation of easy comfort. Forced herself to remember that they weren't lovers any more. He was right, they should go out. It would be a lot easier to remember that they were just good friends if they were in the company of other people, instead of cooped up alone with nothing more exciting than a game of I-spy to distract them. She pushed her hair back from her face. 'I must look like some wild woad-daubed Ancient Briton.'

'You do,' he agreed seriously. 'An Ancient Briton who could do with some lessons in body art.' And she giggled, as she knew she was meant to. Never had anything been so hard. 'You've got twenty minutes.'

Half a dozen towels had appeared in the bathroom. Big, comforting, dark red towels. Emily must have realised she'd need some, Willow thought gratefully, picking one up, holding it to her face. It smelled…it smelled of wood. It smelled just the way Mike had the day he'd brought home that beautiful little table:

not of polished wood, but as if he'd been handling raw, newly sawn timber.

It had been the last evening they'd spent together before the wedding and she'd been brittle with nerves, desperate to pour out her doubts, tell him what was in her heart. She hadn't, certain that it was simply a case of the 'pre-wedding nerves' that every woman famously went through before taking the biggest step of her life.

It would be all right. If she just hung on, it would be all right. Then their hands had brushed as he'd reached for her suitcase packed with her honeymoon clothes so that it would be waiting, with his, at the hotel for them.

Mike had been distracted too and when he'd said he had to go, had things to do, it had almost been a relief. Then his fingers had touched hers and it had been like lighting the blue touch paper. Instant conflagration, urgent, desperate.

And afterwards, her skin had been suffused with the scent of new-cut wood.

She held the towel for a moment, breathing it in, feeling weak with longing for him to hold her again, love her with that same end-of-the-world passion that had taken them somewhere else, a place where ambition, career, the vast, unstoppable momentum of the wedding did not exist. When he'd held her, whispering hot words of love, nothing could touch them.

She dropped the towel as if it scorched her. Emily hadn't brought it. The towels belonged to Mike but they hadn't come from his flat in Melchester. The towels there were blue.

So what? It wasn't her business any more. Except,

standing beneath the hot blast of the shower, she couldn't stop herself from thinking about it. He'd had a home of some kind in Maybridge. It would seem that he still did have one. Had he shared it with someone and that was the reason he'd never talked about it, shrugging off the past as if it didn't matter?

Well, she had news for him. It mattered.

Angrily, she ignored the big, plush towels and used the little tea towels she'd bought, to dry herself, and spent rather more time than she'd intended on making up her face, flicking her hair into place. Then, instead of the nearly clean T-shirt she'd used to dry herself with the night before, and had worn for her shopping trip to the village, she dug out a slate-blue silky knit top that had come out of the drawer with her underwear.

She'd thrown it into her bag, too desperate to get away to bother with sorting silk from cotton. She was glad now because, even when she didn't care what she looked like, a girl needed to have something that she looked good in.

Mike, his hair still damp from the shower, his forearms tanned and sinewy and strong, had never looked more relaxed, more at ease with himself. More desirable. But Willow kept her distance as they crossed the yard to the stile and she clambered over before he could give her hand.

'How far is it across the fields?' she asked.

'About a mile. Just about right to work up an appetite.'

'You speak for yourself, I've been working all day. I've already got an appetite.' Well, she couldn't have him thinking she was pining for him. With luck he'd put her crankiness down to hunger. Again.

She felt him glance at her, knew without looking that a crease would have formed in the wide space between his grey eyes. She knew everything about him. How he looked, how he smiled, how he'd respond when she touched his hand, his shoulder, his face.

But that was superficial stuff. What about inside his head? She realised she knew nothing about what had been going on in there. She had a legitimate reason for running out on her wedding. What demons, what memories, had sent him running from the church?

And what had brought him racing after her?

She kept her gaze fixed firmly on the path ahead of them, moving ahead as the path narrowed, picking up her pace so that they didn't have to struggle for words to fill the silence.

Mike let her go, keeping his distance so as not to crowd her. She was confused. Hell, *he* was confused. He knew in his head that they had done the right thing. But his heart—his big-mouthed heart that didn't know when it was well off—had got him into this mess and now it just refused to let go. He couldn't, wouldn't let her go.

He caught up with her as she reached the kissing gate that led into the lane. 'Hey, what's your hurry? This was supposed to be a stroll, not an endurance test.'

She stepped into the gate, turned and pushed the swinging part towards him, blocking his way.

'Why are you here, Mike?' she demanded.

'Well, I thought we were going to get something to eat.' She said nothing. 'Maybe if you'd let me through the gate—' She took her hands off the top rail and turned swiftly away. 'Willow!' She didn't acknowledge him as he drew level with her. 'I don't know,' he declared. Not true. He knew. He knew that he couldn't marry her, live the life he'd offered her. But he couldn't live without her, either. Still she ignored him and he swung round in front of her, forcing her to stop. 'All right, all right. I didn't think you should be on your own right now.' That, at least, had the merit of honesty. She *shouldn't* be on her own.

'I'm going to have to get used to it.' She walked around him. 'And I'm not sure that you're the person to help me with that. In fact I think it would be a whole lot easier if you left.'

'You want me to go now? Tonight?' She scuffed the ground, kicking at the dust with her shoes as she kept moving, not answering him and suddenly, having provoked a confrontation, she was the one backing off. 'I really should finish the shelves now I've started them,' he said.

'How long will that take?'

He tried not to let his relief show.

'I can't put them up until the kitchen's been painted,' he said casually, as if it didn't matter. 'And Emily asked me if I could build some storage boxes under the big window in the day room. To double up as extra seating.' Okay, so he'd suggested it, not Emily, but he didn't think he'd mention that right now! As they reached the pub, Mike steered her towards a table away from the road. 'Of course if you want me to go, I'm sure she'll understand.'

'I wish I did.'

So did he. Wished he had an answer. But he couldn't be the man she wanted him to be. He'd tried. Waste of time. He should have been concentrating on making her want the man he was. Well, he had a week to do that. 'What can I get you?'

She slid onto the bench, folded her arms on the table and propped her chin on them. 'A gin and tonic. And anything involving mega quantities of calories to eat.' She pulled a face, attempted a smile. 'I'm talking serious cholesterol, here, so you'd better make it a double portion of French fries.'

He waited a minute, sure she would change her mind about that. When she didn't, he said, 'Do you want some salad with that?'

'No thanks. I'm eating for comfort. I want to feel my arteries hardening.'

'You should have said. We could have stayed at the cottages and I'd have made a stack of bacon sandwiches with brown sauce and we could have finished off the chocolate biscuits for pudding.'

'I thought about it,' she said, with every appearance of sincerity. 'Then I thought about what we'd do with the rest of the evening.' She looked up at him, her eyes luminous in the gathering dusk and this time the confrontation had taken on a different edge, something deeper, something more dangerous as she challenged him to admit that the transition from till-death-us-do-part lovers to friends wasn't going to happen overnight. It wasn't going to happen at all if he could help it. 'Tell me, Mike, what do ''just good friends'' do when conversation is limited to the impersonal, and they haven't got as much as a pack of cards to pass the time?'

For a moment his breath seemed to freeze in his body so that he had to force himself to release it, force his mouth into a casual smile. 'I have to admit, you've got me there,' he said as he finally regained control of his thought processes and found the right words. The sensible words. 'Are you sure you're happy to eat out here?'

'We don't have a choice. Your jeans have got paint on them.'

'It's old paint.' She didn't move and he shrugged. 'Okay, I won't be long.'

Willow sat back, watching the comings and goings as cars pulled into the car park, people walking by with their dogs, looking for something to distract her from the pain of what she'd done to herself. What Mike was doing to her. How could he be so casual? So laid back?

A motor cyclist streaked passed, all black leather and crash helmet, exuding danger and excitement as his huge machine leaned into the mini-roundabout where the picturesque thatched village pump stood at what had once been the gossip centre of life in Hinton Marlowe. As she watched, he completed the circle and came back, coming to halt in front of the pub, putting his foot down while he tugged at the strap, then removed the helmet.

Oh, heck.

'Willow. I thought it was you. Enjoying the flesh pots of HM after a hard day with the paintbrush?'

'Jacob.' She managed a smile. 'Finished for the

day?'

'Just about. The shop's been shut for hours, but I've been doing the accounts.'

'Is that what you do when you're not shifting boxes and tending the till? Account?'

'Something like that.' He smiled and she tried harder to look as if she was pleased to see him. Clearly she'd succeeded, because he pulled the bike up onto its rest and walked across to join her. 'Are you on your own? Can I get you a drink?'

'Thanks, but it's being taken care of.'

Mike appeared in the doorway with a couple of glasses. 'The food won't be long,' he said, glancing at the newcomer and then at Willow, waiting for an introduction.

'Mike, this is Jacob Hallam. His aunt runs the village store. He's an accountant, too.'

'Give it up,' Mike advised. 'Get a life.'

Willow stared at him. Then, gathering herself, she said, 'Jacob, Mike is...'

'Mike is getting in the drinks,' he said, cutting off her attempt at anything more elaborate by way of introduction. She let it go. Maybe he wasn't too keen on broadcasting his whereabouts, either. 'Can I get you something? If you're stopping?' He wasn't encouraging.

'Oh, well, a lager, thanks. It's thirsty work, cooking the books.' Mike apparently felt no compulsion to smile.

'We're eating, Jacob. Will you join us?' Willow offered quickly. Mike might not welcome company but she could certainly do with a buffer, an outsider to sop up the growing tension between them. It had been easy to ignore when they'd been working in separate parts of the cottages, but it was now beginning to stretch to twanging point. She moved up, inviting him to join her on the bench.

'Just the lager, thanks. Aunt Lucy will have something waiting for me and she'll fret if I don't eat it.'

As he sat down beside Willow, Mike bit back the urge to tell this leather-clad intruder that it was his place. It wasn't. He'd forfeited any right to the place beside Willow when he'd walked out of church. So, instead of punching the man's lights out, he went and fetched him a lager.

If Jacob could have read his mind, though, he might have got straight back on his motorbike and driven off without drinking it.

CHAPTER FIVE

'ARE you and Mike...?' Jacob left a gap for her to fill in.

'We're friends. Just good friends,' Willow said quickly, testing how it sounded when she tried it on someone neutral. She didn't like it one bit. 'Do you live with your aunt, Jacob?' she said, changing the subject. She was good at small talk, putting people at their ease, discovering their lives. It was what she did, after all, and he responded eagerly, not noticing that she was just going through the motions, had no real interest in his answer.

'Jake, please. And she's not really my aunt. Everyone calls her Aunt Lucy because that's what she is, a sort of universal aunt to the village. She fostered me when no one else would have me.' He grinned. 'I was a bad lad.'

'Yes,' she said, and laughed. 'I'll bet you were.' Still was, given half the chance, she was sure.

'I owe her a lot, which is why I come down and stay whenever she needs me. It gives me a chance to make sure she's still coping. That her accounts are neat and tidy. It's little enough to repay all she did for me.'

'She sounds quite a character.'

'She's a great old lady. Knows every snatch of gossip, knows who needs a hand, a chat, or just a cuddle. The village wouldn't be the same without her. Lord knows what'll happen when she packs it in.' Willow perked up. Human interest. Village community under threat. It would make an interesting feature for *Country Chronicle*… No, no, forget that. The *Globe*. She had to start thinking in terms of what the *Globe* wanted. They'd have a different angle, but still… 'You'll meet her when you come into the shop again. You will come into the shop again?' he added, hopefully.

'I'll make a point of it. I'd really like to meet Aunt Lucy.' She had to get the kitchen painted tomorrow and go over the bits she'd missed in the day room. 'When I'm not up to my elbows in emulsion, I'm a journalist. I'd really like to talk to her about her life, what the village shop means to the community. Would she let me do that, do you think?'

'Aunt Lucy was born to talk. Drop by one afternoon, she'd love to see you. Tomorrow? Tuesday?' Seeing her hesitation, he unzipped a pocket, took out a notebook and wrote down a number and handed it to her. That's my mobile. 'Call me.'

'I'll do that,' she said, tucking the paper into her bag.

He grinned broadly. 'I look forward to it.'

Willow looked up as Mike put a glass down rather sharply in front of Jake Hallam, looking as if he'd much rather tip its contents over the man's head.

Jealous? He was jealous? Did 'just good friends' get jealous?

She glanced at Jake. He was certainly good-looking, but surely Mike knew her too well to believe she'd leap at the first man to make a pass at her simply because their relationship was over?

But when had jealousy ever been rational?

If she'd walked into the bar and found Mike chatting up some pretty airhead blonde, she'd have wanted to scratch the girl's eyes out. And she knew that Mike wasn't interested in airheads, whatever their colouring. At least not during the five months, two weeks, four days that he'd been the centre of her life.

Jake, apparently oblivious to the dangerous undercurrents in the atmosphere, lifted the glass and said, 'Cheers.' Then, after swallowing a mouthful, he said, 'So, Mike, you're part of this painting team are you?'

'Willow's painting. I'm making shelves.'

'I see.' Then, glancing at Willow, he said, 'Maybe I'll come along one evening and pitch in.' It was more question than statement, she thought, testing her enthusiasm for the idea.

'Do you know anything about carpentry?' Mike asked, before she could answer, choosing to take the offer rather more literally than it had been meant.

'Actually I was more interested in painting.' Mike could see exactly what Jacob Hallam was interested in and gripped his glass so hard it was a wonder it didn't disintegrate. 'I couldn't knock a nail in straight to save my life.'

'Why? It's not difficult.'

'We'd really appreciate any help,' Willow intervened quickly, glaring at Mike, even as her heart was doing a joyful little quickstep. Maybe she was shallower than she thought. She *wanted* him to be jealous. Green with it. 'It'll leave me free to get on with the kitchen. The sooner that's done, the sooner you can leave,' she told Mike mischievously and she was rewarded with a demonstration of what exactly was meant by the expression 'if looks could kill'. If looks could kill, Jake would be lying on the ground in urgent need of mouth to mouth resuscitation.

'I'm in no hurry.' Mike was definitely cabbage-green. It was a side of him she'd never seen before. But then, he'd never been challenged for her attention before. Under the circumstances she knew she should be feeling outraged but, instead, she was experiencing a completely illogical hopefulness. Which was ridiculous. 'I won't be going anywhere this week.' He glanced at her, defying her to contradict him. She hadn't the slightest intention of doing so.

'Oh, well, I'll be sure to see you again,' Jake said as he got up. 'Thanks for the drink, Mike. See you, Willow.' He fastened his helmet, then climbed aboard the big, dangerous-looking motorbike, kicked it into life and roared away across the village, to be lost from sight as he turned behind the church.

Mike watched the motorbike leave with a sense of foreboding. Darkly handsome, graceful, dramatic in black leather, Jacob Hallam was the kind of man who only had to flash his eyes at a girl to have her at his feet. And he'd been so casual with Willow, as if he'd known that all he had to do was smile, snap his fingers and she'd be his for the asking.

'Oh, good, here's our food,' Willow said gratefully, when the silence stretched beyond anything that could be described as comfortable, Mike's expression of the kind that would turn milk sour. She smiled at the waitress, assured her everything was fine, since he didn't respond to the girl's query, and picked up her fork. 'Cajun chicken!' she said brightly. 'Good choice. I love—'

'I was wrong, you know.'

'What?' She stopped using her food as a conversational lifeline and looked up. He hadn't even picked up a fork. 'What do you mean, wrong?'

'Yesterday.' Willow held her breath. Wrong to walk out of church? Wrong to walk out on her? 'It wasn't five months, two weeks and four days. It was five. Five days. It's a leap year. I'd forgotten.'

She was unnerved by the depth of her disappointment. Four days, or five days, it didn't matter a hoot. All that mattered was that she loved him and she'd let him go.

'You'd forgotten?' She made herself laugh to cover the tremor in her voice. 'I can't believe you'd ever forget that leap-day feature I did where I talked half a dozen girls into proposing to their boyfriends on the pavement in front of the office,' she said.

'This may come as a terrible shock to you, Willow, but I don't actually read the *Chronicle* from cover to cover.'

He always changed the subject when she talked about the newspaper outside of the office and she'd tried to keep her enthusiasm for her job within acceptable bounds, assuming that local news must bore him. But he didn't even read her features? That was a serious dent in her perception of the way he felt about her. She'd have read a balance sheet to please him.

'Even if you didn't read the feature you must have noticed the increase in advertising revenue,' she pressed. 'We had wedding venues and bridal shops falling over themselves to book space, even offering discounts for wedding services for the six brave ladies involved.'

Maybe her face gave her away, because he found a smile from somewhere.

'I'm sorry, Willow. If I'd made an effort to read more of your fine prose I might have realised how good you are at your job. So,' he said, distracting her from her unhappy thoughts, 'how many of these unfortunate men bowed to the inevitable and accepted the fate you so cavalierly inflicted on them in the pursuit of increased circulation and advertising revenue?'

'All of them.' She glared at him. 'What man is prepared to look like a complete jerk in public?' And he could take that whatever way he chose. Then, because maybe she'd pressured him into making a committment he couldn't live with, she made an effort to justify herself. 'The couples were chosen with a certain amount of forethought, Mike. It was supposed to be light-hearted, a bit of fun.' He didn't seem to find it particularly amusing. 'One of them had been living with his girlfriend for fifteen years,' she said, a little desperately. 'They had three children, for heaven's sake. No one could say he'd been rushed to the altar.'

That got his attention. 'Why would they do that?' he asked. 'Live like that? Doesn't the woman know how few financial rights she'd have? No right to a widow's pension—'

'Once an accountant, always an accountant,' she said. 'An accountant who asked me to move in with him, as I recall.'

'That's not true, you know. At least not in my case.'

'What isn't true?'

'When I asked you to move in with me...' there was a long pause '...I never intended the arrangement to be permanent.'

Well, terrific! 'More, till boredom do us part?'

'No!' Then he said, 'I wasn't thinking that far ahead.'

'Maybe my couple weren't thinking ahead either,' she suggested. 'Maybe it just got to be a habit. I really don't know. But maybe they're right. Maybe the big wedding is all just for public show. Maybe the piece of paper isn't such a big deal.'

'It is, Willow,' he said. 'You know it is.'

'Do I?' She looked up. 'I know that if I'd moved in with you we'd probably be living happily together and I could have taken the job at the *Globe* without it being some huge deal.'

He frowned at that. 'Because you wouldn't have felt the need to discuss it with me?'

'No, because I would have just been your girl-friend. Not the consort to the high panjandrum of Armstrong Publications Ltd, on call twenty-four hours a day, seven days a week with a house full of gold taps needing to be polished, with endless charity dinners to attend, good works a speciality. Because it really wouldn't have been that big a deal.'

She didn't want that? It was the life she'd been brought up to expect...

'Are you sure? You'd have been away five nights a week. Perhaps not always managing to get back at the weekend. What kind of relationship would that be?'

'The kind where you'd have said, ''Take the job if

it makes you happy. It'll make the time we have together truly special.'''

He lifted his shoulders, pushed his head back as if easing a great weight of tension from his neck. 'You're right of course. I knew it. You should have your big break and I was too caught up in my own selfish needs to see it until it was almost too late. My loss.'

'Is that why you walked away from our wedding?'

He straightened, looked her in the eye. 'It would be a comfort to think that my motives were wholly altruistic. But I'm not the man you think I am, Willow. I'm not the man my father wants me to be. I tried. I really tried. I thought having you would be enough to make up for sitting behind a desk all day, manipulating figures, when I had other dreams.' He stopped. 'Then I saw that you had dreams to chase, too. Really, one of us should have had our whole heart in the business, don't you think?'

'I think marriage is tricky enough if both parties are wholeheartedly committed,' she agreed miserably. Just because they were right, she didn't have to be happy about it.

'Did you follow up those leap-year proposals? Do you know how many couples have finally made it to the altar?'

It took a little time to swallow away the aching lump that had formed in her throat. For a moment she felt she'd come very near to what was driving him but, before she could ask him what his dreams were, the shutters had slammed down again. End of conversation. Change of subject. He didn't want to talk to her about his problems, his concerns. He never had.

'Two down, four to go. One of which, I have to admit, is looking very dodgy.'

'Not the couple with the three children I hope.'

'No, they tied the knot the same week. Got a licence and did it without any fuss. They just needed someone to give them a push. Sort out the details, handle the paperwork.' Someone to find out what they had to do. She was good at that. Information was her trade. If you couldn't get answers from one source, you found another. If Michael wouldn't tell her his dreams, she'd find out some other way. There always was some other way.

It might, in the end, hurt even more, but the feeling of having made a decision, having regained control, suddenly made her feel a great deal better.

Then she realised that Mike was still watching her. 'Eat up, Mike,' she said. 'Your chicken will be cold.'

'Comforted?' Mike asked when she finally put her fork down.

'Much better,' she assured him. 'But I think I'm going to need something seriously wicked in the pudding department to complete the cure. What shall it be? Death by Chocolate?'

'Sounds about right.'

She got to her feet. 'My treat. Coffee? Anything to drink?'

'Just coffee. We don't want to get lost on the way back to the cottages.'

'Oh, I think we got lost a while ago, Mike. We were just too busy choosing wallpaper to notice.' She sat down again. 'What are we going to do about the house?' It wasn't something you could just parcel up and send back with thanks and a short note of explanation. 'It's in our joint names, isn't it?'

'Don't worry about it. I'll just need you to sign the deed of transfer some time, so that we can give it back to my father.'

'He'll be so upset. He really loved that house.'

'Yes.' Then he said, 'It was a bit big, don't you think?'

'I guess he hoped we'd grow into it.'

That provoked a somewhat bleak smile. 'We could have had a good time trying.'

She reached across, covered his hand with hers. Then she couldn't think of anything to say that could possibly help so she got up again and went into the pub.

Walking home was a slower process than the rather breathless pace she'd set when they'd started out. It was deep twilight and Willow had no intention of racing on ahead, even if Mike had let her. But as she wove her way through the kissing gate, he caught her hand.

'Wait,' he said. 'Wait for me.' And she waited.

She wasn't walking along that path, in front or behind him, on her own. There were too many unidentified noises, squeaks and scrapes and scurryings in the hedgerow. Maybe that was why she left her hand in his. Why she gripped it so hard, when away across the field where the ground rose to a small copse she heard a long, agonised cry that goosed her skin.

'What on earth was that?'

'A rabbit. The weasel eats tonight.'

Her hand flew to her mouth. 'Oh, that's…'

'The food chain in action,' he said gently as she

turned to him, buried her face in his T-shirt. Rabbits, beetles, one excuse was as good as another.

Mike held her. It would be so easy to keep holding her, kiss her, forget the nightmare of the last few days. He sensed instinctively that, whether she acknowledged it or not, she wanted that too. They were close to the cottages. One kiss would be all that it took and then they'd be running for it, ripping off their clothes as they tumbled through the door. But then what?

Beneath his hand, her pulse was racing, but no more than his own. Just to hold her, breathe in the scent of her hair, tightened the hot coil of desire, the need to have her in his arms, to possess her. She was clinging to him as if to a lifeline and some reckless part of him was urging him to go for it, self-destruct.

She'd never forgive him. He'd never forgive himself. He fought the temptation. This time he promised himself, he'd get it right. This time it would be different.

This time? Who did he think he was kidding? There wasn't going to be any 'this time'.

Except that somehow he had to make it happen.

The how of it was beyond him right now. So he just held her, waiting for her heart rate to return to normal, waiting for her to regain her composure.

'I'm sorry,' she said, pulling back a little self-consciously when it became obvious that he wasn't going to take the opportunity she'd given him any further. 'In my world rabbits are cute, cuddly things on birthday cards, not some sharp-toothed creature's dinner...' She wiped a single tear from beneath her eye that had nothing to do with the rabbit. 'Lord, how pathetic am I?'

'Not pathetic. Empathetic.' And he rewarded himself with a comforting kiss to her forehead before he put his arm around her shoulders and walked her home. He unlocked the door, turned on the light. 'You go ahead,' he said, as she turned to see why he hadn't followed her. 'I'll just look around, make sure all the outbuildings are secure.'

She lingered in the doorway, back-lit by the kitchen light, her face in darkness. 'Mike…' Her voice was as full of uncertainty and need as his own heart. They had been lovers until yesterday. What had changed, after all? Take it back a couple of months to the moment before he'd proposed… And suddenly he saw the point she'd tried to make about the job not mattering. There was only one problem with that: he didn't want to go back to a point where it didn't matter.

His proposal might have been provoked by her unwillingness to move in with him, but the feelings he'd had that night were as strong as ever. He wanted to wake with her beside him every morning for the rest of his life. Nothing else would do.

'I'll see you in the morning, Willow.'

He knew she'd wanted him. Willow covered her cheeks with her hands. She'd thrown herself at him like a dehydrated duck diving into a muddy puddle. And he'd rejected her.

All that made her embarrassment bearable was her certainty that he hadn't found it easy to walk away. Why else would he have decided to stay outside, checking up on the outbuildings, putting himself beyond temptation?

This wasn't about a lack of desire, a lack of need for each other. That was as strong as it ever had been. It was about more fundamental problems that they hadn't ever addressed.

She turned on her phone in case he'd sent a message. Nothing. She keyed in *'Help!'*

Then erased it.

Maybridge. That was where she'd find the answers to the questions that had kept her awake all night long. Willow stood back to get a better view of the wall she'd spent the morning retouching, but it wasn't the paint job that occupied her. It was Maybridge.

'You've done a good job.' She turned as Mike joined her. 'Coffee?'

'Mmm, thanks.' She took the mug and quickly looked back at the wall. His bare, sweat-slicked torso was far too exciting for ten o'clock on a Monday morning. Far too exciting for a relationship that had run its course and was going nowhere. 'It's a bit bare, don't you think?' Then she blushed, but Mike didn't appear to notice her confusion as he stood back and contemplated her work.

'It could do with something to break up all that blue,' he said after a moment. 'A few clouds, maybe.' There was something about the way he said it that made her look back at him.

'Into every life a little rain must fall?'

'It seems to work that way, although I think the kids who come here will have probably experienced a deluge rather than a shower. Maybe they'd prefer a big smiley sun.'

'If we had both,' she pointed out, 'we could have a rainbow.'

'For hope?'

'We all need cartloads of that.' But what, exactly, was she hoping for? 'A bright green hill with some daisies would be good, too,' she said quickly, before the eager little brain cells, positively panting with hope, urged her to fling herself at him, tell him that she'd made a mistake, and didn't care about her career, only about him. Unfortunately, she wasn't the only one who'd decided at the last moment that plighting their troth wasn't such a great idea.

'Just to be sure we keep our feet on the ground?' he enquired, with the slightest hint of irony.

'I think we're probably the most grounded people in a hundred-mile radius.' Why else would she be having such a civilised conversation with a man who'd jilted her? Who she'd jilted? 'Maybe we should have a little hot-air balloon.' She sipped her coffee. 'Drifting over the hill.'

'Why don't you get Jacob onto it? I'm sure he'd be happy to oblige with all the hot air you can take.'

She restricted her response to a smile. Jealousy was good. Jealousy meant he cared. She couldn't believe how much she wanted him to care…

'I'd better check with Emily before I get carried away with the representational art. Meanwhile, I have to make a start on the kitchen if you're ever going to get out of here,' she said, unable to resist pushing the little green buttons a little harder.

'No, first you have to drink your coffee. Bring it outside and get the smell of paint out of your lungs,' he said, steering her towards the door. 'You can tell me what you think of the shelves. Gently,' he warned, as she reached out to run a finger along the smooth finish. 'They're just fitted together, not glued and screwed.'

'I had no idea,' Willow said, taking in the scope of the project. 'I thought you were making some little shelf unit to hang on the wall. This will fill the whole of that end wall, won't it?' She glanced up at him. Then she said, 'I love the way you've smoothed out the sharp edges.'

'Kids horse around.'

'It's all so clean, so professional. I didn't know you could do this stuff.'

'I didn't know you'd applied for a job on the *Globe.*'

She spun round. 'But I did that before I met you.'

'Ditto,' he said. Then, when she was quite lost for words, he stepped back, tossed the dregs of his coffee into the grass and put down the mug. 'I'll need some more timber if I'm going to make a start on the storage seating.'

'Yes.' Her mouth felt like glue. 'And I need to make some phone calls. The girl at the *Globe* told me to call Toby Townsend today.'

'From St Lucia?' he asked, a dangerous edge to his voice.

'No, of course not—'

'Don't be defensive, Willow. A career girl has to make these sacrifices, even on her honeymoon.' His voice dripped with sarcasm. 'Or maybe even last week you were beginning to have doubts about where your best interests might lie?' Then he shrugged awkwardly. 'I'm sorry. I don't blame you, really. I didn't exactly respond like a "new man" to your big chance, did I?'

'Not exactly. And correct me if I'm wrong, but I don't believe your flight from commitment was the result of a sudden blinding flash of insight at the chancel steps. Was it?'

'Not entirely.'

When he didn't elaborate, she carried on. 'The only reason Toby is expecting a call from me this morning is because he was out when I rang last week. His assistant said I should call today and it seemed easier to say yes than go into details...' That did sound defensive. And details would have been a heck of a lot easier than this. 'So I wrote a letter,' she added lamely. She had no reason to feel bad. But she did. She felt terrible.

'And now you have to phone and explain that it was all a mistake. That you didn't mean it. I guess it's been that kind of week.'

'Actually the letter never got sent.' Oh, hell! 'It was on the hall table with a stamp, just waiting for someone to go to the box.' Then she lifted her shoulders and dropped them again. 'I picked it up from the hall table as I rushed out of my parent's house on Saturday.'

'That was quick thinking under pressure. I'm impressed.'

'Well, I can hardly come back and work at the *Chronicle*, can I?'

'You can do what you like, Willow, I won't be there.'

'Won't you? Why not?'

'But maybe it would be a good idea to call and let

someone know your plans. They'll need to find someone to replace you.'

'And you?'

'Yes,' he said, after a moment. 'And me.'

'Replacing your son and heir is rather different
from replacing a reporter, Mike.'

'You can't resign as a son, Willow. I've tried. At
least, I've tried to resign the heir bit. I think this time
I might have managed to convince the old man. I'm
just sorry you got caught in the crossfire.' Mike
picked up a wide pine plank, the muscles in his back
standing out as he turned away from her. 'Well, what
are you waiting for?' he asked when she didn't move.
'Hadn't you better get on with it?'

'Yes.' She had so many questions, and now just
the glimmer of an answer, but he couldn't have made
his position clearer. He didn't want to talk about it.
'I'll call Toby right now.'

And then what? If she was going into London—
if?—she'd need clothes. She glanced down at herself.
Proper clothes. The kind of clothes that suited her
new image as a journalist on a national newspaper.
Sharp and sexy. But she couldn't face the prospect of
going back to her flat, creeping in, avoiding the neigh-
bours. Avoiding her mother, who probably had the
place staked out.

Maybe Crysse would have calmed down sufficiently to consider bringing her some stuff. Or maybe
even to meet her and help her choose something new.
Her casual, comfortable regional-newspaper image
would probably make her look like a country cousin
in the *Globe's* London office.

Besides, she really needed to talk to Crysse, try to

explain about changing her mind. But when she dialled the number, despite the fact it was the school holiday, there was no answer, not even from the answering machine which would at least have provided the comfort of her cousin's voice.

Talking to Toby Townsend, delighted as he was to get her call, eager as he was to see her, didn't do a thing to lift her spirits. She consoled herself with the vigorous application of white paint to the kitchen wall.

'You're beginning to get the hang of that,' Mike said when he came in to wash his hands at the sink. Perched high on a stepladder, reminding herself that this was her choice, trying to convince herself that she'd done the right thing, she merely grunted. 'It's a pity you didn't start at the other end, though. I could have installed the shelves this evening.'

'Oh, heck. I wasn't thinking.' Or maybe she was. She wasn't anywhere near as eager for him to leave as her mouth kept saying she was. 'I'll do that wall next, then, shall I?'

Mike shook his head. 'No, don't get out of your rhythm. I can carry on with the boxes for now.' He wiped his hands on one of the red towels that had found its way down from the bathroom. 'It's your turn to make lunch, by the way.'

'Is it? Who posted a rota?' she asked, then realised that he might have a point. So far he and Emily had provided all the food. 'I'll open a couple of cans. Soup, or beans on toast?'

Mike leaned back against the sink, arms folded, looking up at her. 'You're not at your best in the kitchen are you, Willow?'

'That depends what I'm doing in it.'

He ignored her attempt to make him laugh. 'Admit it, you hate cooking.'

'You're wrong. I don't hate it, I've just never seemed to be able to quite get the hang of it. All that rubbing in and whipping up...' A spatter of paint hit her cheek and Willow gratefully seized this opportunity to deal with a totally unnecessary blush by wiping the drips from her face with the sleeve of her T-shirt. 'All that washing up.' Then she said, 'Oh, I get it! It was the appalling prospect of having to cook your own Sunday lunch that sent you running from the church. Admit it!' She could change the subject with the best of them. Mike, rather than owning up, disappeared behind a cupboard door. 'What are you doing?'

'Getting lunch before I starve to death. You've talked me into it.'

'Works every time,' she said flippantly. Her thoughts did not match the lightness of her voice, however. What on earth was so desperate that he couldn't face talking about it? Hadn't he learned anything about not talking? Hadn't she? 'I'll have the soup,' she added, propping her brush on the paint tin, stripping off the rubber gloves and climbing down from the stepladder. 'With toast. Five minutes?'

'Five minutes.'

She picked up her bag. 'Just time to wash and brush up.'

Upstairs, with the bathroom door shut, she extracted her mobile phone and switched it on.

'Directory enquiries, how can I help you?'

'I'm looking for a Maybridge number. Michael Armstrong.'

'Do you have an address?'

'No, I was hoping you might be able to give me one.'

'I'm sorry, we can't do that.'

'Oh, well, the number will have to do.'

A recording clicked in and she made a note of the number. It didn't mean anything of course. He would have had a Maybridge number before he returned to Melchester. Nevertheless she dialled it and got a recording.

'You've reached Michael Armstrong Designs. The workshop is closed at present, but if you leave your name and number I'll get back to you,' Michael's voice assured her. She disconnected as if stung.

CHAPTER SIX

MICHAEL Armstrong Designs? Willow sat there in a daze.

She had no idea what she'd expected. Michael Armstrong, Accounts R Us, maybe. But *Designs*? A *workshop*? What on earth did he design? Business systems? Software? Did that require a 'workshop'?

Far from getting answers, she had even more questions. She needed a local business directory, she needed to go to Maybridge, she needed—

A sharp rap on the door startled her so much that she dropped her phone.

'Willow? Are you okay? I've been calling.'

'Fine,' she said quickly. 'I'm fine. Sorry.' She retrieved her phone and stuffed it in her bag, dragged her fingers through her hair and quickly washed her hands.

Mike was waiting for her on the landing when she emerged and his brows met in a quick frown. 'Is something wrong?'

'No.' She thought her face might crack as she smiled. 'What could be wrong?' The man she'd been about to marry had a life she knew nothing about. What could possibly be wrong with that?

'You look a bit pale. Maybe it's the paint fumes. Why don't you give it a rest this afternoon?'

'I intend to.' She moved her arm before he could touch her. She was familiar with that tender little gesture. She loved the caring way he would rub his hand over her arm, look into her eyes, his eyes crinkling at the corners as he smiled and then kissed away whatever bothered her. Kissed away questions. Not this time. She was going to get to the truth; she was going to confront him with it and then she was going to move into the pub until he'd finished making those damned shelves. 'I'm going to London tomorrow to meet with my new boss and I need something suitably sharp to wear. I'm going shopping this afternoon.' In Maybridge.

There was the slightest pause. 'Do you need company?'

'Are you offering to give me the benefit of your advice on the most suitable, um...*design*?' she asked. She wanted to scream.

'I was offering to drive you,' he returned mildly. 'You're on your own in the fitting room.' Then a slow smile lifted his features. 'Belay that last remark. I'm more than happy to help with the hooks and eyes—'

'Thanks, but you've forfeited any rights to play with my hooks and eyes. Besides, you've got plenty to keep you busy here. I called Crysse.' Well, she had called her. It wasn't a lie. Then, because she didn't want him making a fuss, insisting on coming along, since she was so *pale*, she said, 'She's meeting me.' Which was the biggest, fattest lie she'd ever told.

'Crysse?' he repeated dully, clearly far from reassured. She wished she'd said nothing, but it was too late now.

'Who else?' she demanded defensively.

After a moment he stepped back to let her pass. 'If you're sure.'

'I'm sure. And don't worry about dinner,' she said quickly as she clattered down the wooden stairs. 'I'll get a cooked ready meal to heat through. I may be useless at producing my own haute cuisine, but I'm an absolute whizz at heating through someone else's.'

'Willow...' She turned at the foot of the stairs, made an impatient gesture when he hesitated. 'It's been a tough few days. Don't do anything you might...' He seemed lost for words.

'What?'

'Regret.'

Regret? As far as he was concerned she was going to buy a new suit. If she regretted it, she'd change it. But he looked so tense...

'Don't worry, Mike. I think I demonstrated my capacity for avoidance of regret on Saturday. We both did.' Her attempt at a careless laugh echoed around the unfurnished house, sounding brittle and unconvincing.

'No.' He joined her at the foot of the stairs. 'I mean it. I've hurt you, I know that. I'd give anything to change what happened, to have done it all differently but, please, don't make it worse by doing something stupid.'

He sounded so serious that she shook her head. 'Don't worry about me, Michael. I'm in need of a little retail therapy, that's all. Stupid will be restricted to the impulse purchase of a suede purple miniskirt when I should be buying something classic in black.'

'Really?'

'Wrong answer. You're supposed to say "You'd look terrific in a purple miniskirt."'

'You'd look terrific in a purple miniskirt,' he said,

but he wasn't laughing. 'Just don't get tempted by anything in black leather.'

'I never wear—' The words died in her throat as he reached out, cradled her cheek for a moment, his hand shaking slightly, or maybe she was the one who was shaking, as he slowly lowered his mouth to hers. It was like his first kiss. His first touch. Hesitant. Full of questions. Do you want this? Are you feeling this? As if we're on the edge of an abyss and that, if we step off, there'll be no going back.

It was like that. But different. Tender and loving rather than the urgent, sensuous prelude to passion. His mouth was gentle, his kiss had a sweetness that left her on the edge of tears.

'What was that all about?' she demanded, blinking furiously, when after all too brief a moment he straightened, looked at her as if imprinting her face on his memory.

'I want you to remember that what we had was special.'

A dozen scathing remarks leapt to her lips, but she had the feeling that they were talking on different wavelengths. The one point of contact that remained was that kiss. It wasn't much to keep her warm as she rose through the stratosphere to the icy heights of success.

So she bit back the angry words and instead put her hand briefly over his. 'Yes, Mike. It was.' Then, as she realised they had both spoken in the past tense, she turned quickly and stumbled towards the kitchen. It was over. The trip to Maybridge was a waste of time. But she still had to know.

The creamy soup slid, without too much difficulty,

down a throat that felt as congested as the M25 in the rush hour. But she couldn't manage the toast. Mike must have lost his appetite because he didn't bother with it either.

Mike watched her drive away in her little yellow car, then he took his cellphone from the rear pocket of his jeans and punched in a number. 'Cal? Did you do what I asked?' he demanded, before the man could speak. 'Did they go?'

'Eventually. Crysse was too distraught to make any kind of decision but Sean finally persuaded her that getting away would be a good idea. Where are you? How—'

'I'll call you later.' Mike switched off. It wasn't conversation he was looking for but confirmation. Willow had lied to him about shopping with Crysse. He'd known it. He hadn't wanted to believe it, but it was true. His hand tightened around the telephone; he wanted to smash it against the wall, smash the shelves, smash the boxes.

He was good at that. Smashing hopes, smashing dreams. This time he'd managed to do it to himself and now he knew how it felt.

It hurt.

He'd come after Willow with some crazy idea of starting over. Beginning again, showing her who he really was, convincing her that they could make it if they both tried. He still wanted her so much that it hurt.

But, instead of telling her that, he was letting her drive away to spend the afternoon locked in the arms of a man whose seduction routine was as slick as his black leather biker gear.

And worse was to come. She'd come back later, brittle and bright to hide her misery at what she'd done, or happy and contented as a kitten—he couldn't begin to decide which would be worse—and pretend that nothing had happened. Chatter about shopping and how she just hadn't been able to find a thing she liked.

He dragged his hands over his face, pushed his fingers through his hair. He'd wanted to regain control of his life, give her back control of hers. But she hadn't waited for him to act. She didn't need him to give her anything. She'd taken it. Maybe he should accept that and leave before she returned.

Willow stopped at the village store. Aunt Lucy would have a business directory. It took a while. Jake had warned her that the lady was born to talk; he hadn't been kidding. But after promising to come back later in the week for a *real* talk, she finally got the information she was looking for and managed to escape.

Mike wiped his arm across his forehead. He'd spent half an hour in a frenzy of activity, determined to finish the cabinet-making—anyone could paint the shelves and boxes—determined to forget about Willow and what she was doing. All he knew was that she hadn't gone shopping with her cousin and that he didn't want to be here when she came back with hot, shining eyes.

He picked up a bottle of water, drank from it, then poured the rest over his head. It cooled him down.

This was crazy. He was driving himself crazy. He had her tried and convicted without a shred of evidence that she'd gone to spend the afternoon with Jacob Hallam. Apart from their flirting at the pub. Apart from the fact that she'd locked herself in the bathroom before lunch to make a phone call.

As Emily rounded the corner of the cottages, he headed for the four-by-four. 'I've got to go out,' he told her as she stopped alongside him.

'Yes, but—'

'Lock up if I'm not back. I've got a key.'

He didn't have time to explain. It was time to stop worrying about what he should do. He knew what he had to do. He had to catch his runaway bride and tell her that he loved her, that he'd always love her. Then, maybe, they could start working out a future that they could both live with.

The old lady who ran the shop looked up as he burst through the door. 'Yes, dear? Can I help you?'

'Is Jacob Hallam here?'

'Oh, no, I'm sorry, but you've missed him.'

His chest tightened painfully. 'Do you know where he's gone?'

'London. A board meeting. He's such a busy lad these days, dashing about on that bike of his. But he promised me he wouldn't go over the speed limit.' Mike thought she was living in cloud-cuckoo-land if she believed anyone with a motorbike that could do a hundred and thirty miles an hour would be keeping to seventy on the motorway. But he didn't disillusion her. 'He'll be back later though. He's going to give that nice young lady a hand painting her house.'

'Willow?'

'Oh, do you know her, too? I was telling her just now, Jacob was a bit of bad lad in his youth, but I knew all he needed was a chance.' She smiled fondly. 'These days he's all heart.'

'Willow was here?'

'Yes, dear. She's going to write an article about the shop. I can't think who'd be interested, but she seemed very keen. Not that she had time to talk today. She just stopped by to check something in my business directory.' It was still open on the counter and Mike put his hand on it before she could close it and put it away. It was open at 'A' and there was a tiny spot of ink where Willow had grounded her pen. Right alongside the listing for Michael Armstrong Designs.

Maybridge was a lively town with a booming industrial techno-park, but it had a much older heart left over from its market-town agricultural beginnings.

Willow pulled into the parking area at the rear of a vast rambling building that had once been an old coaching inn, but which had now been converted into accommodation for small craft shops, with office accommodation above. This was it?

She looked at the long list of occupants on the board in the main entrance but Mike's name wasn't there. She turned to the receptionist. 'I'm looking for Michael Armstrong Designs,' she said.

'Outside, through the carriage arch.'

'Thanks.'

'But he's not there. The workshop's closed—' the girl called after her. Willow waved her acknowledgement. She knew he wasn't there. It was all she did know and as she followed the arrow, her heart was booming like a kettledrum.

Her first impression was of flowers. Hanging baskets trailing lush and brilliant summer flowers. And in the corner, a flower shop spilled out into the courtyard with buckets of lilies and roses that lit up the shady corner.

There was a boutique to one side, with sharp, witty clothes in the window. There was an aromatherapy centre, painted glossy black with the name Amaryllis Jones picked out in gold. And a tiny jeweller's studio with individual pieces on display in a small window.

She instantly recognised the hand that had worked the exquisite engagement ring Mike had given her. A wide, misted band of platinum with a diamond at its heart. Why hadn't he brought her here, let her meet the person who had made her ring? What was he hiding?

Willow turned to confront the mystery.

The far side of the courtyard was totally occupied by Michael Armstrong Designs, housed in what had once been the carriage and stable block, high enough for a hayloft and quarters for the groom above.

The entrance was through enormous double doors, with a smaller, personnel door, set into it. Both parts were shut, with a 'Closed until further notice' sign hanging lopsidedly from a horseshoe mounted on the smaller door.

She crossed the yard and, standing on tiptoe, pressed her face against the high windows, feeling excluded, shut out.

'Can I help you?' Willow turned guiltily to find herself facing a tall young woman, her fairness ac-

centuated by her black clothes. Her green eyes inde-
scribably vivid. 'I saw you from over there. I'm
Amaryllis Jones,' she said, waving in the direction of
the aromatherapy centre. Then, perhaps used to dis-
belief, she added, 'Most people are kind and just call
me Amy. You're looking for Mike,' she said. Not a
question.

'Yes. I am.' Not his body, but his soul. His spirit.

'I've no idea when he'll be back. I dropped by to
say hello when I saw the lights on a few days ago,
but he wasn't in the mood for company. He's closing
up the workshop.' Amy shook her head. 'He had go
home and run the family business when his father was
taken ill. And he's getting married. Maybe his new
wife will expect something a bit grander than this?'
That did sound like a question. One that went straight
to Willow's heart. Amy had made it sound as if any
woman who wanted more than this wasn't truly wor-
thy of him. Maybe she was right. 'Sarah—she has the
clothes shop—said she saw him yesterday when he
stopped by to pick up some stuff from the flat.'

'Flat? He lives here?'

'You didn't know?' She looked up at the row of
long, narrow windows that ran horizontally just below
the roof. 'It was just a hayloft when he moved in. He
converted it himself.'

'It's to let, you say?' Willow crossed her fingers
behind her back. 'It could be just what I'm looking
for. Does anyone hold a key?'

'You really should go through the agent. There was
a sign, but it seems to have disappeared—'

'But I'm here now,' she pointed out. 'No point in

bothering the agent if it isn't what I'm looking for. Is there?'

'None whatsoever.' Amy Jones smiled, fetched a key and unlocked the door, pushing it open and standing back to let Willow through. 'I think you'll fit in here very well.'

Willow's forehead wrinkled in the slightest frown but, before she could ask why Amy thought that, she saw the drawing and took a step forward. It was pinned to a corkboard over the workbench, a sketch and a working drawing. It was the design for the table Mike had given her.

She crossed the workshop, reached out, touched it, traced the lines he'd drawn.

'That was the last piece Mike made. I saw it the other day when he was putting the finishing touches to it. The man is a poet in wood.'

'Yes. Yes, he is.' And she wanted to weep. How could he have made something like that and given it to her and never told her that he had made it with his own hands?

'He's got a waiting list for anything he cares to make. Of course it takes him weeks to turn out one piece of furniture.'

'Yes, I can see that it would.' What was it he'd said? Something about it not being a business for a family man. Maybe not. No man who worked like this would ever be rich. But he'd never be poor, either—not in spirit. She looked around. This was his dream and he'd been prepared to give it up for her.

No wonder, when she'd told him about the job she'd been offered, he'd seemed so cool. It must have seemed to him that she was giving nothing, just demanding more and more.

If only he'd told her.

If only she'd seen.

'This is the workshop and there's a small office at the end. It's pretty big. Would you need this much space? What do you do?'

'Do?'

'She paints.' Mike's voice jolted her from a deep and lonely pit of regret and she spun round. 'Isn't that right, Willow?'

'Mike…'

Amy laid the key on the table. 'I won't be needing this any more. Will I?' She stepped out through the door and closed it behind her.

Mike was leaning, arms crossed, against the door frame. He was waiting for an answer, too. The difference was, Mike wasn't going anywhere.

For a moment Willow's mouth opened and closed, as her brain freewheeled. Then, as the penny dropped, she demanded, 'Did you follow me?'

'You lied about meeting your cousin,' he countered. 'Have you seen enough down here?' Then, while she was still trying to gather up her mouth, chivvy her thoughts into line, he unlocked the door to the upstairs apartment, exposing a spiral timber staircase to the upper floor, and stood back to let her go first.

She wanted to go. Curiosity was clawing at her insides, but she stayed where she was.

'How did you know that I wasn't meeting Crysse?'

'I'm psychic.'

'You *did* follow me.' She couldn't believe he could be so sneaky. 'Why?'

'Because Crysse and Sean are in St Lucia.'

'What?'

'After we talked at the motorway services, I couldn't quite bring myself to claim the cancellation insurance. It didn't seem exactly ethical under the circumstances.' He smiled. He really shouldn't do that. It went to her head like champagne and stopped her thinking straight. 'I thought perhaps Crysse might need to get away. Do you mind?'

Mind? She was stunned, but mind... 'No. No of course not. It was a wonderful thing to do.'

'So why did you say you were meeting her?'

'For a psychic you ask a heck of a lot of questions.'

'Humour me.'

'You wanted to come shopping with me. I wanted to...' She did a quick mental word search for an alternative to 'snoop'.

'Do a little research?' he offered, perceiving her difficulty.

That sounded better, but there was no hiding the fact. 'I think probably snooping says it better.'

'I see.' And he smiled again. 'Willow Blake, Investigative Journalist.'

'You see nothing,' she said crossly. 'I shouldn't have been reduced to this. Why didn't you tell me, Mike?'

'Shall we go upstairs?' She didn't move. 'This is going to take a while.'

'I'm glad we're in agreement about that,' she said. 'That's a starting place. But you can't hustle me out of here. I want to see everything. I want to know everything.' She turned and looked up the design pinned to the corkboard, not quite able to trust herself to keep up the cool act if she continued to look at him. She was so angry. So unhappy. So…sad. How could he have hidden this from her? Pretended? 'Did you make that for me, or was it just surplus to requirements?' she asked. She couldn't believe that was her voice. She sounded so distant. So cold.

'No.'

She spun round. 'No *what*?'

'I didn't make it for you. I made it before I met you. I was working on it when I had the call that my father had been taken ill.' He moved to her side, unpinned the design and laid it on the bench, smoothing it out with his hands. 'It was a development piece. A new design. It was sitting here when I came last week to shut up the workshop, waiting for the final polish.' She was very still. 'I thought, well, what's one afternoon stolen from a lifetime? So I polished it. Finished it so that there would be no loose ends lying around to trip me, bring me down.'

'Last week?' This was where he'd been when she'd gone to his office, seeking reassurance. 'I was looking for you. I even wrote a text message to ask you where you were. The way you used to send them to me. Remember?' Mike heard the change in her voice. The sharp challenge had become softly wistful. 'The way you did on Saturday night.'

'I remember,' he said. 'It would seem I've lost the touch.'

She shook her head. 'Not just you. Both of us.'

'I didn't get your message.'

'I didn't send it. Maybe I sensed that it was all

slipping away from us.' She looked up at him. 'Would you have answered me? Told me where you were?'

'Probably not.'

'No, I didn't think so. And I could never have guessed, could I?' She shivered, looked around. 'What is all this machinery? What does it do?'

'Cut, plane, turn.' He took her through the workshop, explaining each process, answering her questions as if she was visiting royalty.

'And your designs?' she asked. 'If I wanted to commission you to make a piece of furniture for me?'

'Willow—'

'Please. I want to know everything.'

'I'm trying to tell you. It's difficult.'

'I know, but I'm listening. Just follow my lead. Tell me about your designs.'

He opened up a plan chest, took out a folio of designs, photographs of finished pieces. She flipped through them. 'You really made all these?'

'Yes.'

'This?' she asked, staring at a picture of a small desk.

'It was commissioned by Fergus Kavanagh. The man who gave the Trust the cottages. For his wife.'

She glanced up at him. He said it as if it was nothing. 'How much would it cost to buy a desk like this from you?' He mentioned a figure and she drew in a sharp breath. 'That's a lot of money.'

'It took a long time. And I can only make one at time.'

'You work on your own? No assistants? No apprentices?'

'I didn't want the responsibility.' He shook his head. 'Maybe I knew, one day, I'd have to give this up, go back.'

'You'd be wrong to. The *Chronicle* could never compete with this.' The *Chronicle* couldn't compete, but it had a better claim on his loyalty than some selfish girl who put her own needs first, she realised. 'When did you know?'

'That I couldn't give it up?'

'No, when did you know that this was what you wanted to do?'

'Oh, I see. At school. I was supposed to be doing Latin, but I just couldn't stay out of the workshop. The scent of wood pulled me in like hot cakes fresh out of the oven. I typed out a letter on my father's notepaper giving permission for me to swop. I don't think my tutor was fooled, but since I wasn't ever going to an intellectual asset to the classical languages department he took the pragmatic view that learning some basic workshop skills would be of more use to me than Latin verbs. Once I'd made my first project, I was hooked.'

'And then you went to university and took business and accountancy? Why?'

'Because my father asked me to. I wanted to take a hands-on course in furniture design. He thought I was mad, that it was something I'd grow out of, or that I could take up as a hobby if I was really keen, but he was far too clever to say so. He suggested that business management and accountancy would be useful.' He shrugged. 'It seemed to make sense—'

'And if you still wanted to study furniture design?'

'He promised he'd support me.' Mike shrugged.

'And meanwhile I was visiting museums, galleries, working with craftsmen when I could get them to take me seriously. Learning all the time. When I graduated he asked me to do a year at the *Chronicle*. It was the family business; I had a duty to the people who worked for him. I should know how it was run.' He looked down. 'When I realised that every capitulation simply fed his conviction that sooner or later he would win, I walked away.'

'You came here?'

He looked around. 'There was a preservation order on this place, but it was a wreck. No one wanted it. I took it on, raised some money, traded help with restoration in return for long-term cheap rents for shops, offices. I learned one hell of a lot about solid, basic carpentry and, what do you know? My father was right, the business and accountancy degree was a real help.

'You own this place? All of it?'

'The bank and I have an agreement. So long as I keep paying them money each month, they allow me to believe I do.' He stood back, held open the door to the upper floor. 'Do you want to see where I lived before I met you?'

'Not lived. Live. You're coming back, aren't you? You're never going back to the newspaper?'

'Never's a long time. I said that once before, but I went back when my father needed me.' He thought about it for a moment. 'I'd do it again, but only while I looked for a buyer for the paper.' He saw her expression. 'You think I'm wrong?'

'There's been an Armstrong Publications in Melchester since the days of moveable type.'

'Yes, I know and I wish things were different. I wish I could be the son he needs. The husband you had a right to expect me to be. I tried, I really tried, but my heart wasn't in it.'

'Then you're right to walk away. A newspaper, a newspaper like the *Chronicle*, must have heart.'

'I'm just beginning to realise that.' He glanced at her. 'You won't find much of that in evidence at the *Globe*.' When she didn't respond, he extended his hand. 'Shall we continue the tour?'

Willow knew she shouldn't take it, shouldn't take that short flight of stairs to his other world. She knew that what she'd see would break her heart.

But nothing in the world could have stopped her.

CHAPTER SEVEN

WILLOW climbed the spiral staircase to the upper floor knowing that the apartment would be special. Nothing could have prepared her for the elegance, the simplicity, the economy of the home that Mike had fashioned from the old hayloft.

'It's lovely, Mike.' It was more than that. It was all she had ever wanted. Small, everything within reach just about, uncluttered, a place to live in rather than live up to. A total contrast to the vast, demanding house in Melchester that had been waiting to suck her up, absorb her, turn her into its slave.

The floor was a wide expanse of pale, polished wood, the fittings all clean lines and function, the soft furnishings a rich dark red that she recognised instantly from the towels he'd brought to the cottages.

Willow knew he was watching her as she walked slowly through the place he'd made with his own hands. Her hand trailed along the rounded edge of the simple screen dividing the living area from a raised sleeping space. She took two steps up the ladder to where a thick mattress was installed on a platform beneath a huge, angled skylight.

'This is...cosy.' Her mouth was dry but she had to say something.

'It was the only way I could fit in the shower room. It's quite something lying under the skylight on a frosty night.'

There was a pause that seemed to go on for ever while Mike wondered what she'd say if he invited her to stay and try it out. While Willow wondered what she'd say if he asked her.

'It must be like sleeping beneath the sky,' she said finally. She glanced down at him.

'Better. No matter how cold it is outside, it's warm beneath the covers.' He smiled briefly. 'And when it rains you don't get wet.'

Right now she could think of nothing she'd like better than to climb up there, burrow down beneath the quilt with Mike and stay there for a week. Pure self-indulgence.

A week or a month, their problems would still be waiting.

She backed down the steps and followed the smooth, curved transition from the white and steel shower room and on into the kind of galley kitchen that featured in lifestyle magazines. Her fingers recognised the work. He'd made all this. Mike had made this and it was beautiful.

'Why didn't you tell me?' she asked again.

'That I was a carpenter by inclination, a managing director only by duty? The truth?'

She thought his description of himself as a carpenter was disingenuous. A carpenter was a craftsman, a man who made windows, doors, a thousand artefacts for everyday living. Mike was an artist. She turned to him. 'The whole truth, Mike,' she warned. 'I'm not interested in the edited highlights.'

'You won't like it.'

'I don't expect to. That's why you didn't tell me about any of this before. But if you don't want me to walk out of here right now, you don't have any choice.'

She waited, breathing on hold, until he nodded. Then she dropped her bag, curled up on a huge sofa, her legs tucked beneath her, and waited.

Mike glanced at the space beside her and, choosing the wiser option, took the armchair facing her, stretching out his long legs, scraping his fingers through hair that immediately flopped back over his forehead. Putting off the moment.

At last, he said, 'I didn't tell you because I knew Willow Blake wouldn't be interested in a man who made his living with his hands.'

'You're right.' He stilled, paled as he met her steady gaze. That encouraged her a little. Her reaction was important to him. 'I don't like it. Not one bit. Where do you get off judging me like that?' Then, when he didn't immediately answer, she realised her optimism was misplaced. It was worse, much worse than that. 'It wasn't just that, was it? You didn't bother to tell me because you didn't take our relationship seriously. Here today, gone tomorrow. Thanks for the memories.' Willow was shaking, trembling, and she drew her knees up beneath her chin and wrapped her arms around her legs.

He didn't defend himself. There was no real defence. She was basically right on both counts. 'It started like that,' he admitted. 'Isn't that how all relationships start? Chase and kiss. Kiss and chase.'

'Ours ended like that too. Tell me about the middle.'

'You mean the part where I took myself by surprise and fell in love with you—'

'Don't say that! You don't love me! You lied to me. You lied about who you were!'

'The part where I realised I couldn't live without you.'

'Skip to the part where you suddenly realised you could live without me,' she said bitterly. 'Did you mean it when you asked me to marry you?'

'Yes, damn it, of course I meant it.' He leaned forward, his elbows on his thighs, his fingers still raking restlessly through his hair. Then, because he hadn't been the only one with doubts, he looked up. 'You said yes. Did you mean that?'

Willow wanted to fling herself at him, shake him for being so stupid, but there was only one way that could end and one of them being stupid at a time was more than enough. 'I think I'd like a drink,' she said, her voice shaking from the emotional turmoil she was putting herself through. But she needed answers. All of them.

'Tea, coffee? It'll have to be black—'

'I think this situation calls for something stronger than tea.'

Mike didn't argue. They were both driving, but a drink would mean she would have to stay, give him precious time to try and explain. He opened a cupboard, took out a couple of glasses and a bottle and poured out two large measures of brandy. As he pressed a glass into her hand, she fumbled it and he realised that her fingers were icy despite the heat.

He took her hands and wrapped them carefully around the glass and held them there for a moment until he was sure she was in control. Because touching her was what he wanted to do most in the world. Touch her, hold her, tell her he loved her.

That would be self-indulgence of the worst kind. He'd told her that he loved her. Now he had to *show* her. So he let go of her fingers and sat down beside her, lifted her feet onto his lap. 'You're cold.'

'Yes.' She sipped the brandy and shivered. And didn't actually object when he sat beside her, took her feet onto his lap and began kneading some warmth into them.

It was easier, talking without having to confront a pair of blue eyes that demanded his soul on a plate. 'You're right of course. At first I didn't think our relationship would matter. I didn't plan on hanging around long enough for it to matter.'

'That is honest—to the point of brutality.'

'And since being managing director, even just an acting one, gave me a totally unfair advantage over the opposition within the company—'

'You really are a—'

'I know,' he said. 'I know. But it backfired on me. Big time. You had this image of me, this expectation. What was I to say? Hey, big surprise, Willow, you thought you were getting the CEO of a seriously profitable company…now come and see what I really do.'

'I wish you had.' Her voice wavered and she took another tiny sip of brandy.

'I'm sorry, Willow. I made a mess of it and I'm truly sorry.'

'So am I,' she said. 'I was ready to trust you with the rest of my life…'

Truth. She demanded it, but so did he. 'Only until you had a better offer,' he said, but very gently.

'It wasn't that simple.'

'No, my love, it never is.'

'I wish you'd told me. Right at the beginning. Brought me here.'

Mike thought about how it would have been with Willow in his arms and nothing between them and the stars but a sheet of glass. 'So do I.'

'You should have trusted me.' And she pulled her feet away.

He felt utterly sickened by the mess he'd made of her life and of his. 'I made assumptions about you that were wrong. Totally wrong. Cal warned me. He saw...but I thought you were just marking time at your job until you found the right man to marry.' She looked up from the pale golden spirit pooled in the bottom of her glass and stared at him. 'Someone with the right name, or the right background. Someone from your own circle.'

'Oh, *right*.' She was seriously offended. 'And I was busy congratulating myself only yesterday that you weren't interested in airheads. It never occurred to me that you saw me as one.'

'I don't. You aren't. Except...'

Her eyebrows rose a notch. 'Except?' The slow, quiet manner in which she repeated the word did not leave him with the impression that she was calm about any exception. Far from it. 'You've started, Mike. Please finish. I can't wait to find out exactly how I've convinced you that I have nothing between my ears but sawdust.'

He hadn't said that. He didn't think it. They both knew it. But there was no retreat. 'Whenever I came looking for you in the office, you always seemed to be covering some charity fashion show, or the ladies' lunch club, or the local point-to-point meeting…' he was remembering exactly how he'd found her at a point-to-point meeting, champagne in one hand, a bunch of Hooray Henrys hanging on her every word '…all that social, county stuff. It's your world.'

'What if it is? I got sent to cover those events because people knew me, or least they knew my mother, they trust me, they talk to me because they've known me since I was in my cradle. I've also spent time out on the street with runaway kids, covered life in a woman's refuge, Saturday night in casualty. Maybe you were busy those days?' She didn't wait for him to answer. 'I don't just do fluff.'

'Valentine's Day wasn't fluff?'

She flushed angrily. 'Damn it, Mike, that's seasonal fun. I didn't believe you when you said you never read the paper. Clearly I should have taken that statement seriously.'

'It wasn't… I didn't… I thought if I stuck to administration, distanced myself, I wouldn't get drawn in…' It was hopeless. How could she begin to understand? 'I wouldn't be the first to fall for the siren song of family tradition. It's hard to resist when everyone thinks you're just being stubborn. That you'll come round. When your mother calls and says, "Please…I need you to do this for me…"' He looked at her, hoping that she could read his sincerity in his eyes. 'When there's no one else.'

'Dear God, Mike, you were going to be running the thing for the rest of your life if you'd married me. That *is* what you're saying? You were going to sacrifice the life you wanted—not for family tradition, or your mother, but for *me*?'

'Yes.'

'Idiot!'

'Cal didn't think so. He—'

'I'm not interested in what your best man thinks! I want to know why you didn't tell me!'

'I was working on it. I was going to bring you here, put the whole thing on the line, tell you everything. Then my father gave us the house and I could see how much you loved it, how much you wanted it—' Her explosive interjection suggested otherwise. 'Except for the taps,' he said.

'This just gets worse.'

He found a wry smile from somewhere. 'I didn't believe that was possible.'

'Trust me, it is. I *hated* that house, Mike.'

'Oh, come on, you don't have to pretend. I remember every moment of that day. You were over the moon with excitement. You said, "I can't believe it. This is more than I can take in. I don't know what to say. I'm overwhelmed."' He wickedly imitated the thrilled voice that she'd used to cover her anguish. 'Every one of your words, believe me, is indelibly imprinted on my mind.'

'Then maybe you should have spent a little less time working on your impersonation of me and a little more time thinking about what the words were actually *telling* you.'

'I saw you, Willow. And let's face it, you'd have changed the taps in a second—'

'The taps. That dear little niche in the hall. The reproduction Adam fireplace, the carriage lamps outside… You're missing the point here. These are details. It wasn't you I was running away from. It was that house and everything it stood for. I am not a domesticated woman, and that house…well, it was right out of a 1950s Doris Day movie.'

'You were pretending? But why?'

She put down her glass. She didn't need brandy, she needed Mike to see where she was coming from.

'Your father had just given us half-a-million-pounds-worth of house, Mike. Was I supposed to say, Actually, Mr Armstrong, I know you mean well but you've got lousy taste and I wouldn't live in this house if you paid me? I was brought up to be polite. To say thank you when someone gives you anything, even a lousy rotten juicer that makes you feel as if you've surrendered the life you dreamed of and are beginning to live your worst nightmare.'

He stared at her, for a moment totally lost for words. 'The juicer, too?' He wanted to laugh. Fortunately, he didn't.

'How could you have done that to me? Put that burden on me? No wonder you've seemed distant. You were distant. You were a million miles from me.' She struggled out of the soft embrace of the sofa, stuffing her feet into her shoes. She had to get out of there, go somewhere she could have the howling, miserable weeping fit that she'd been putting off since Saturday. 'I don't blame you for taking off the way you did. You must have hated me…' Her voice broke and he caught her, wrapped his arms around her, pulled her back to hold her close.

'Sweetheart, please. I don't hate you. I could never hate you.'

She wouldn't surrender, but remained stiff and unyielding, her back to him. 'You didn't trust me. You don't know me at all.'

'I loved you. I just wanted you to be happy.'

Loved. He said loved. Willow's heart seemed to crumple inside her as she turned and pushed him away. Despite everything, if he'd said 'love'—present tense—they might still have been able to rescue their relationship from the rubbish cart before it got hauled off to the tip. But 'loved'—well, that told her exactly where she existed in the scale of his priorities.

'Happiness requires security. For that I need a man I can trust, a man I can believe in—whatever job he does. I'm sorry to have to report that you've failed. In all departments.' She headed for the stairs.

'*All* departments?'

She caught her breath. How dared he reduce what they had to that! 'Marriage isn't just sex. Marriage is for better, for worse. Richer and poorer, the whole works. Marriage is like diamonds. For ever.' She pulled the zip on her bag and took out the ring he'd given her. She put it down on the shelf beside her. 'Learn the lesson, Mike. Next time make sure you're honest—'

'There won't be a next time. I just wish—' She had her hand on the door. 'I just wish I'd told you about all this. You were right, we could have had it all. We still could. Don't go.'

She turned slowly. He was an arm's length away. All the temptation a girl could want. It felt exactly like that moment when he'd asked her to stay, asked her to live with him, asked her to marry him.

'I was wrong about that, Mike. No one can ever

have it all. There are always sacrifices to be made. Sharing someone else's life takes all the heart you have and then some. You have to be prepared to give more than you get back. Maybe that's why Crysse, despite everything, is still with Sean. She loves him enough.'

'Then, Sean's a bigger fool than I took him for.' Willow refused to comment on who was the fool. 'If I asked you now, what would you say?'

'Asked me what?'

'Asked you to marry me, Willow. Just the two of us, with a couple of witnesses, no fuss, no frills. No cake.'

No, 'I love you'? No, 'I'm sorry I made such a mess of the whole thing.'? No compromise?

The sun was slanting in through the high windows highlighting tiny dust motes, sparking rainbows off the heavy glasses with the barely touched brandy. There was the indentation of their bodies on the sofa. The scent of wood.

And there was Mike. Tall, strong, golden haired. He was everything she'd ever wanted and she knew that if she lost him, her heart would shatter irretrievably. She'd been so certain that he was the man she was destined to spend her life with. Somewhere inside her a tiny spark of hope told her that it was still possible. But if she'd learned one thing from the first time he proposed, it was that wanting to say 'yes' was not necessarily a great reason for saying it. That their relationship had been built on sand and needed to be rebuilt from the ground up. On the rock of truth.

'No thanks,' she said.

Maybe she'd taken too long making up her mind

because he didn't seem entirely convinced. 'Is that a permanent no thanks? Or an "I'll think about it" no thanks? Or even a "Don't be cheap" no thanks?'

'It's a "We've got two lives that don't converge" no thanks,' she replied.

'You mean, I've got some more work to do?'

She wanted a big career in journalism. He wanted to make beautiful furniture in Maybridge. Each of them knew what they wanted for themselves. They had to work out whether they were strong enough to fit those two ambitions into one shared life. It wasn't going to be easy. It was probably a recipe for disaster. It would undoubtedly be wiser to leave things as they were.

'It means,' she said slowly, acknowledging that they had both made mistakes, 'that we both have.'

'We have to work out what we can't live without? And what we're prepared to let go so that we can be together?' he persisted.

He'd got it. And now they could both see why it was impossible. 'I really do have to go and buy something to wear for my meeting with Toby Townsend tomorrow.'

'The London job is not up for negotiation, then?'

'Is Maybridge?' Even as she said it she knew it wasn't the same. She didn't want him to give up Maybridge whereas he found the idea of her working in London...difficult. If the sacrifice wasn't equal, would one of them feel cheated? She wished Crysse was home so that she could talk to her. She'd cried, but she hadn't been ready to give up on Sean. Then, pausing in the doorway, something else snagged at the back of her mind and she turned back. 'What, exactly, have you got against black leather?'

'Black leather?' He looked distinctly uncomfortable.

'Yes, black leather.'

'I really hoped you'd have forgotten I said that.' Which just made her all the more curious. 'I thought you were coming out to meet Jacob Hallam,' he said when she stood there waiting for him to answer her question. Willow considered what he'd said for a moment, but before she could react he reached out, his hand stopping a millimetre from her arm. 'It's why I followed you.'

Jealous.

She suddenly felt a rush of warmth for this big, lovely man who had tried so hard to change his life for her. How could she have doubted that he loved her? That wasn't sand. That was rock through and through.

Not that she was letting him off. Jealousy was bad. Following her was bad. She could scarcely stop herself from grinning.

'To save me from making a "big mistake"?' She emphasised the words by making little quotation marks with her fingers. 'What were you going to do? Snatch me from the jaws of temptation? Hit him?' She knew it was unfair to ask. Yes, or no, he couldn't win.

'All of the above.'

She was wrong. That did it for her. 'How did you work out where I was going?' she asked; she had to do something to stop herself from flinging herself at him, dragging him up that ladder and restarting the honeymoon without the benefit of church.

'I didn't. I stopped by the village shop to see if Hallam was there. Hoping that he was there.' He couldn't quite meet her gaze, she noticed. Embarrassed. It just got better and better. 'Maybe you should take him up on his offer of a date. According to Aunt Lucy he was at a board meeting in London—a lot more your style than this.' He gestured around him.

'You leave me to worry about my style,' she said, ignoring the slightly off note in his voice. Jake was no competition for him but if he didn't know that now, she wasn't going to put him right. Laid back, she loved him. Protective and jealous, he made her feel... 'Date?' she queried. 'What date?'

'Didn't he ask you out on a date when he turned up at the pub? I heard him ask you to call him,' he prompted.

'Oh, *right*,' she said. 'Yes, he did, and I meant to—' His head snapped back as if she'd hit him. Enough. 'It was to arrange a time to talk to Aunt Lucy. I wanted to interview her, talk about her life in the village, the shop. The countryside is hot news right now.'

'Oh. I seem to be the one making "big mistakes".' He repeated her quotes gesture. 'Wholesale.'

'There's a lot of it about,' she conceded. Then she said, 'You haven't answered my question, Mike. How did you know where I was going?'

'It wasn't difficult. You left a pen mark by my entry in the directory.'

'Michael Armstrong, Private Investigator.' She

pulled in her lips as she tried not to smile. Pumping Aunt Lucy for information wouldn't have been difficult. His big problem would have been getting her to stop so that he could get away and use it. She cleared her throat. 'I really do have to go…shopping… Are you going back to the cottages?'

'I have to. The shelves. You?'

She nodded. 'See you later, then. Do you want me to bring food?'

'No. I'll cook.' He led the way down the stairs. 'Or we could go out. We haven't had a date since…' his eyes darkened '…since I gave you that table.'

She flushed. 'It's okay. You can cook,' she said, rather more crisply than she was feeling. She was feeling that another moment under those grey eyes and she'd melt.

He was smiling slightly as he opened the door for her, as if he knew it. He probably did. 'You're sure you don't need any help with the hooks and eyes?'

'I'm a big girl, Mike,' she said, stepping through into the courtyard, glad of the shade to cool her down. 'I've been dressing myself since I was four years old.'

'So? You learn to do it yourself and you get this terrific sense of accomplishment, which is just great. Then you learn that it's fun to let someone help. Which is a whole lot better.'

'Just as long as it's not Jake?'

'You've got it.' He stepped out after her. 'Come on, I'll take you over to meet Sarah. She makes exciting clothes. I wanted to bring you here…' He let that go. 'I'll bet she'd even be able to find you a suede purple miniskirt if you're still feeling reckless.'

'But no black leather,' she said, refusing to admit

how she was feeling at that moment. The sudden charge of desire was making all that sensible, let's-get-this-right determination dissolve, melt away under the jump-start flash of his hot grey eyes.

'Purple leather would be okay.' He grinned. 'With matching knee-high boots.'

Willow thought that if Sarah had anything remotely resembling that particular combination in her boutique, she might just toss her good intentions to the four winds and let herself be recklessly, irredeemably tempted.

Amaryllis stopped them as they passed the door of her tiny emporium, and handed Willow a small carrier. 'They're candles. You'll need them tonight.'

'Will we? How do you know?'

'Trust me. I'm an aromatherapist.'

Willow glanced uncertainly at Mike. 'That's what she says. Actually, she's a witch,' he said, almost believing it. There was something about Amy that always made Mike vaguely uneasy. He had the feeling that she knew it and that it amused her. 'But she's right. You can trust her. She knows everything.'

He took the bag, opened it. There were a dozen or so candles made to float in a dish, or a pond. Willow peered over his shoulder and sniffed appreciatively.

'What is that?'

'Palmarosa,' Amy told her. 'To alleviate emotional disharmony. And Rose otto, to soothe negative feelings.'

'If the electricity goes out we'll need all of that,' Mike said. 'Any suggestions regarding food?' he asked drily. He glanced at Willow. 'Or we could still eat out?'

'Smoked salmon,' Amy suggested. 'Avocado. Peaches.' She never took her eyes off Willow and, after a slight pause, she smiled and added, 'Dark chocolate.'

Willow sighed with pleasure. 'I'm not arguing with that.'

Maybe it was the scent of the candles, or Willow's eager anticipation of her favourite foods, picked with unerring accuracy by his unsettling tenant, but Mike found himself smiling, too. 'If we have a power cut tonight, Amy, I'll look out for you flying home on your broomstick.'

'Actually, Mike, I usually take the bus.' Her brows twitched mischievously in Willow's direction, then she bent to pick up a small black cat that appeared at her feet.

Mike left Willow with Sarah and, after a visit to the nearest supermarket, he headed back to the cottages. His slightly euphoric mood was dashed by the discovery that Jacob Hallam had returned from London and was now upstairs with Emily, keeping his promise to help with the decorating.

'Hello, Mike. Willow not with you?' he asked casually, as he paused to recharge his roller. Casual wasn't fooling Mike. The man had one reason and one reason only for giving up his time this way.

'She's shopping. I didn't expect you today. Aunt Lucy said you were up in town.'

'I was. Turn your back for a minute and someone starts a takeover rumour.' Mike stared at him. He was *that* Jake Hallam? Software magnate at twenty-five…

'But, hey, what's a rumour when kids need a place like this.'

'You didn't have to rush back, we'd have managed.'

'Really? You don't appear to have been doing that well according to the *Evening Post*.'

'Oh, great. What are they saying? No. Don't tell me—'

'I thought I'd better fill him in on the details,' Emily said, adding pointedly, 'that you and Willow have holed up here while you sort things out.'

'Are you sorting things out?'

'We're getting there. Which is why I know you'll understand why I'd be grateful if both of you were somewhere else when the sun goes down.'

Jake lifted the roller from the tray, but paused before applying it to the wall. 'You've got it. In fact if you get it right I'll stand as godfather to your first-born.'

There was an element of challenge in that statement that Mike couldn't let pass. 'And if I get it wrong?'

He grinned. 'Maybe I'll ask you to return the favour.' Mike didn't think, he reacted, slamming Jake back against the wall. 'Hey, mind the paint—'

'You mind your own damned paint. And *I'll* mind Willow.'

Pinned against the wall, Jake just grinned. 'Good reflexes. It's a pity your brain isn't working at the same speed.'

'What?' The red haze cleared and Mike took in with horror the way his hands were bunched around the man's shirt front. The mess he'd made of the newly painted wall.

'I was just kidding, Mike. Anyone who knows me will tell you, I'm not the settling-down type.'

He released the man. 'Emily...Jake...I'm so sorry.'

But Emily was grinning, too. He couldn't understand why they found it so funny. 'Don't be. I love it when a man isn't afraid to show exactly how he feels about a woman.'

'Just don't forget to let Willow know, too,' Jake said. 'And save me a place at the font. I might not be into marriage but, I promise you, I'm a great godfather.'

Mike's reaction to the thought of Willow with his baby in her arms was so utterly overwhelming that he couldn't answer. Instead he retreated to the kitchen and spent what was left of the afternoon installing the shelves and thinking about what Willow had said. Trying to think of some way that they could both have what they wanted and still be together. Wondering how she felt about having a baby. She'd need a year or two to establish herself first.

He could wait.

The hell he could.

CHAPTER EIGHT

'THE shelves look wonderful, Mike.' Willow dropped the glossy carriers containing her new clothes and crossed to have a closer look. 'Are they finished?'

'They just need painting. I'll do it tomorrow when you're in London.'

She looked around. 'Where is everyone? I expected the place to be buzzing by now.'

'Jake Hallam had a date.' It was probably true. 'And I've a feeling that Emily might just be putting people off so we can be alone. I feel guilty about that, she looked exhausted.' Definitely true. 'So I gave her a bar of your favourite chocolate and sent her home to put her feet up.' He grinned at her expression. 'Don't worry, there's another one in the fridge. You've been an age. Did you find an outfit to impress your new boss?'

'That was the easy bit. Then I needed shoes, and a bag and underwear—'

'Underwear? I thought you'd already got the job—' He backed off hurriedly as she advanced on him. 'Hey, I was just kidding!' She kept coming. 'Really! The first thing I do when I get a new suit is hunt down matching boxers...'

Her scowl disintegrated into a giggle that made him want to just grab her and hug her and never let her go. 'Sarah was terrific; and afterwards Amy made us all a cup of camomile and honey tea. Very soothing.

156

I really like her, Mike. She's…' Willow shrugged. 'I don't know. There's just something about her.'

'Hmm. Are you hungry?'

'Not desperately. A glass of cold white wine would be good, though.' She opened the fridge door, took out a bottle of perfectly chilled wine and handed it to him. Then she snapped off two squares of cold chocolate. She handed one to Mike and let the other dissolve on her tongue. 'Heaven,' she said.

'That was supposed to be after dinner chocolate.'

'Oh, don't worry, I'll have some more after dinner,' she assured him, gathering her bags and heading for the stairs. 'Why don't you open the wine while I go and hang this over a door. We can sit outside and drink it and watch the stars come out.'

'And light Amy's candles?'

Candles glimmering in the twilight were the stuff of romance, Willow thought, when what they needed was light, a hundred and fifty watts of it, bright enough to illuminate every corner of their relationship. She paused, her hand on the door latch.

'You don't really believe there's going to be a power cut, do you?' she asked, evading the question. She yearned for the candles.

'No chance. It's summer, light half the night and warm enough to sleep outside. Power cuts come in the middle of the winter when there's snow on the ground, it's pitch dark for fifteen hours out of twenty-four and all you want is non-stop soup and hot-water bottles.'

'Of course. She must have made a mistake.'

Mike heard the catch of disappointment in

Willow's voice as she turned away, and listened to what it was telling him.

And he thought about what Amy had actually said when she'd given them the candles—*'you'll need them'*—that was all. They'd instantly assumed she'd meant a power cut, when what she'd meant was they would *need* them.

A mistake? 'Not necessarily, sweetheart,' he murmured, as Willow headed upstairs. 'Not necessarily.'

Willow shook out the suit she'd bought for her meeting with Toby Townsend. The skirt was short, the jacket long, the whole effect was city-slicker smart. He couldn't fail to be impressed.

Which was great.

This was the opportunity of a lifetime. Not a moment for second thoughts. She'd already done the second thoughts bit. Her career was where she wanted it to be. It was the rest of her life that was in turmoil.

She took a shower and was towelling her hair dry at the window, hoping that the gold edged wisps of cloud might inspire her. But life wasn't like that. If you let life just happen, depended on dreams, you might end up with nightmares.

Planning was what made dreams come true.

Well, she had a plan. It wasn't perfect, but maybe Mike would be prepared to give it a chance. She combed through her hair and headed downstairs.

The kitchen was empty. The wine had gone. 'Mike?'

Nothing.

She opened the fridge. The food had gone, too. Even the chocolate. A very grown up game of hide and seek? Grinning, she took out her phone and tapped in, 'Where are you, Mike?'

She didn't have to wait long for an answer. 'You can have me if you can find me.'

Promises, promises. 'No clues?'

'Follow your nose.'

Nose? Scent? The candles. She looked around but Amy's gorgeous little black and gold carrier had gone too. She went to the door and stepped out into the gathering twilight. A few yards away she saw a candle sitting on the path. She picked it up, held it to her nose. Rose otto. To soothe negative emotions.

Actually, there was nothing negative about her feelings for Mike. She was very positive that she wanted him. Right now. She looked around and spotted another candle, at the end of the yard, and a third on the path to the old, walled orchard.

She hadn't been in there, but Emily had pointed it out to her from the window of the cottages. She'd gone on at great length about how they planned to convert it into a safe-play environment for the children, as if afraid that her volunteer, if left in silence for more than a minute, would dissolve into hysterics.

She opened the old door set into the wall and on the slightest breeze she caught the scent of newly crushed grass, and something more, that was like an old and pleasing memory.

'Am I getting warm?' she sent.

'You tell me.'

Oh, yes. She was warm and getting warmer by the second. She picked up another candle. Palmarosa, this time. To alleviate emotional disharmony. She sat on the trunk of a fallen tree, letting the scent develop in her hand. There had been disharmony. A lot of it. Now everything seemed quite clear. The phone beeped again.

'Well?'

She smiled. He was getting impatient. She liked that. She liked that a lot.

'Getting hotter by the yard,' she told him.

The trail of candles led through the orchard to a small pond. Mike was sitting with his back propped up against an old weeping willow, its trailing leaves stirring in the dark water. His eyes were closed, his cellphone held loosely in his fingers. He tossed it onto the soft grass.

'What kept you?' he said.

'Getting there is half the fun, Mike. The anticipation, the waiting.'

His lids lifted to reveal a gleam of silver-grey beneath his lashes. 'That sounds promising.'

She sank down beside him, letting the candles fall in a heap between them. 'Do you have any matches?'

He produced a box from his pocket, opened it and struck one. 'You see? I'm prepared for every eventuality.'

Red-hot. Burning.

He picked up one of the candles, lit it, then rolled over, stretched out on his stomach, leaning over the edge of the pool to set it adrift.

She lay beside him, holding another for him to light. The wick caught and she held it in the water for a moment, sheltering the flame until it grew tall and steady, making her fingers baby-pink and transparent. The water was cold, the scent sweet, the air utterly still as Mike lit the remainder of the candles and sent them out into the centre of the pool.

'Magic,' she said.

'Did you make a wish?' he asked.

'No.' She glanced at him. 'Did you?'

'I prefer to think that I'm in control of my own destiny. Ready for that drink?'

He reached for the bottle and a couple of glasses. 'Glasses?' she queried.

'I brought them from home. I'm tired of the taste of plastic.'

Willow had no answer to that, instead she sipped the lush, buttery chardonnay Mike had bought and watched the flickering flames grow brighter as the night gathered about them.

'Wouldn't life be simple if we could stay here for ever?' Willow said finally, rolling over onto her back.

'Life *is* simple. It's people who are complicated.' He glanced at her. 'I've been thinking—'

'Dangerous on an empty stomach.' Willow didn't want to get involved in complications right now. She just wanted a beautiful, simple evening, that would go with her beautiful, simple idea. 'I was promised smoked salmon.'

For a moment he looked as if he was ready to push it. Then he shrugged and sat up. 'Smoked salmon,' he said, reaching into a carrier. 'Bread,' he said, tearing a small flat loaf in two. 'And cream cheese.' He handed her a knife.

'Avocado?'

'Help yourself,' he said, waving at the bag.

'Cherries?'

'The peaches were hard.'

'This is perfect.'

They had eaten the bread and Willow had settled against the crook of Mike's body, his warmth at her back, his arm looped around her waist as he fed her sweet, dark cherries.

'You're perfect,' he said. 'I briefly lost sight of why I was prepared to give up everything for you. Today…' Mike remembered exactly how he'd felt when Jake Hallam had challenged him, when he'd been forced to confront his deepest desires, recognise what he was in danger of losing, understand how it would feel to see Willow with his child at her breast. 'Today I discovered that nothing in the world was worth that.'

'I know.' She turned in his arms. 'It's all right, Mike. I've worked it out.' And because she knew her solution wasn't perfect, because she didn't want any arguments, she leaned into him and kissed him with her cherry-stained lips.

'Willow—'

'Love me, Mike,' she murmured, her tongue sweet against his. 'Love me now.' Once he'd made love to her, he wouldn't be able to walk away, say no.

Mike wanted nothing else at that moment. Just to love her. It was why he'd chosen this secluded spot, with its lush grass. He'd had one thing on his mind and with her in his arms he knew that the world was well lost…

In his arms, there was a chance she might agree with him. But it wouldn't be enough, he wanted more than that. He wanted more than this night to remember.

'Willow, sweetheart, wait…we need to talk…'

She looked at him, her eyes reflecting the candle flames. And she smiled. 'Later,' she said, and her mouth sizzled against his throat as she straddled him and began to slip the buttons on his shirt, pushing it back so that her hair brushed softly against his naked shoulders. 'We'll talk later.'

Now. They should talk first, but it wasn't easy to hold that thought with Willow's hands embarking on a seductive raid of his senses. With her hands cool against his hot skin, her mouth intent on distraction, a man could be forgiven for letting his priorities slip a little.

His hands slid beneath the hem of her T-shirt, spread across the satin-smooth skin of her back. He encountered her bra, unfastened it, and with a single easy, unhurried movement, pulled T-shirt and underwear over her head. Then, as his fingers stroked across her shoulders, sliding down to cup her breasts in his hands, she smiled at him and said, 'Now, what were you saying?'

She was right. It would keep. 'You're wearing too many clothes,' he growled softly.

'Wrong. But hold that thought.' And there was a flash of white teeth as she briefly smiled.

'*I'm* wearing too many clothes?' he offered. She shook her head, her eyes intent. He'd lost his appetite for conversation. Lost his appetite for games. There was only one thing he wanted to say and now was the moment. 'I love you, Willow. I want to marry you.'

She swallowed, her eyes gleamed moistly as if she were on the point of tears. No need for tears... 'You're getting warmer.'

'Believe me, I'm on fire—'

'Back up a place.'

Back up. What the hell…? Then he got it. 'You want to live with me?'

'There.' She blinked. 'That wasn't so difficult was it?'

'No.' It wasn't difficult. It was where he'd started, after all. And now he understood her reaction to his initial proposal. He'd discovered the need for commitment. Total commitment. 'No,' he repeated, letting his hands slide down the length of her body until they rested at her waist. She waited for him to undo the button. Gave an impatient little wriggle. He tightened his grip to keep her still; if she wasn't still he'd explode with his need for her. 'I don't think you understand, Willow. I said, no. Thanks.'

Willow frowned. Then didn't need his hands to keep her still. She shivered. 'Mike, it's what you wanted. You said…'

'You convinced me that I was wrong. Moving in with someone says nothing. Unlike marriage it's an estate entered into lightly. What we have is worth more than that. It demands the taking and giving of vows. Till death us do part. I asked you to marry me. What happened to the, ''We'll work on it''?'

How could he do this? Ruin everything? 'Don't you see, Mike? This makes sense. I'll have a flat in London, you'll have your place in Maybridge. We could have weekends together. You could come to London sometimes. We'd have three, maybe four nights a week together.'

'It's an interesting concept. Five out of ten for trying, but it needs more work. Tomorrow. Now, shall we get back to the clothes thing?'

'Clothes thing?'

'"Hold that thought" you said. I'm on hold, but I'm not made of stone, baby…'

The heat rushed to her cheeks and Willow pulled back. Mike didn't make any attempt to stop her as she turned away, grabbed for her T-shirt and tugged it over her head. She had never been so humiliated in her life. How could he have done that to her?

No. She wasn't blaming Mike. She'd done this to herself!

Beside her, lost somewhere in the long grass, her phone began to ring. She'd been avoiding taking calls for days, but suddenly anything was better than meeting his gaze and she scrabbled around until she found it, punched the receive button. 'Yes!' she snapped.

'Willow?'

'Crysse!'

'Willow I've got something to tell you,' she rushed on quickly. 'It's so difficult…' Crysse was crying.

'Darling, what is it? What's wrong?'

'Nothing. Nothing at all. It's perfect. Would be perfect if you were here. We're in St Lucia—'

'I know. It's brilliant. Are you having a great time?'

'The best. Except…I don't know how to tell you this.'

'Say the words, Crysse. Just say the words.'

'Sean asked me to marry him. Here. We're getting married here at the weekend…'

Willow's mouth was working, but nothing was coming out.

'What is it?' Mike demanded, sitting up beside her.

'Crysse and Sean...' Her mouth was dry. 'They're getting married.'

'Willow?' Crysse whispered.

'Sorry, darling, I was telling Mike your news.'

'Mike? You're back together? Ohmigod! You'll come! You'll both come! Sean wanted him to be best man, but I said he couldn't possibly ask—'

Mike heard, took the phone from Willow's lifeless fingers. 'Crysse, when is it...? We'll be there... I'll call Sean tomorrow... Absolutely... And congratulations.'

Willow put out her hand to him and he took it. 'Thank you.'

'What for?'

'You did that. I can't tell you what it means to me—' And because, for a moment, talking was difficult, she squeezed his hand. 'Thank you.' She shivered. Sniffed. Kept her face averted. 'It's getting cold. The candles are going out.'

'And you've got a big day tomorrow.'

'Yes.' Big day. Big deal. She tugged at her hand, but he held onto it.

'Willow?' He pulled her back towards him. 'Are you crying?'

She dashed away a tear that trickled down her cheek. 'No, of course not. Why would I be crying?'

'From happiness?' He took a handkerchief from his pocket, dabbed at her eyes. 'Either that or you've sprung a leak.'

Her lips trembled on a smile. 'Don't!'

'What?' he said innocently.

'Make me laugh.'

'Wouldn't dream of it. Here.' And he put his arm around her, drew her against him. 'You have a good cry if you want to. It'll make you feel better.'

For a moment he thought she was going to succumb to the temptation to let out all the bottled up anguish of the last few days. For a moment he felt like joining her. But then she recovered her poise sufficiently to get to her feet. Mike followed suit and she looked at him.

'Are you sure you don't mind doing this for Sean?'

'Hell, no. It's my duty. And if he gets cold feet at the last minute, you can be sure I won't advise him to head for the hills the way my best man did. I can tell him, from firsthand experience, that the only thing to do is stay put and work it out.'

'I suppose I should say I'd do the same for Crysse. Except she isn't as stupid as me.'

'You're not stupid. I was the stupid one.' She would have argued with him, but he turned her around and gave her a little push in the direction of the cottages. 'Go. I'll clear up here.' She walked a few paces, looked back uncertainly. 'I'll call you in plenty of time in the morning.'

'We need to make arrangements, tell people—'

'You can leave all that to me.'

'At least we won't have to pack,' she said.

'No, we won't have to pack.' Their suitcases were all ready. Waiting for the honeymoon that hadn't happened.

She walked slowly back to the cottages. She needed Mike. Wanted him beside her, holding her, but he was right. They needed to sort out exactly where they were going. What they wanted. More importantly she needed to sort out some things with her family. Make her peace with her mother. She took a deep breath and made the call.

'Mum? It's Willow. I'm sorry—'

Mike cleared up the remains of their picnic, then leaned against the tree, trying to think of some way to sort out their future, make it possible. After a while, the navy blue darkness was punctuated by a square of yellow light as Willow switched on a light upstairs in her room. He imagined her preparing for her big day, lunch with Toby Townsend at the *Globe*. She deserved a chance at the big time. He didn't think she'd enjoy it that much, find much heart up there, but she needed to find that out for herself.

That heart was everything.

He took out his cellphone, keyed in a number. 'Dad? It's Mike. I'm sorry—'

'How was it?' Mike had called her at the *Globe*, told her not to come back to the cottages but to meet him at Heathrow, at the check-in desk. He had picked up her suitcase, her passport.

'Different,' she said. 'Frenetic. Crowded.' She thought of the way everyone had been crammed into a huge open-plan space, with scarcely room to swing a cat. They had a cat at the *Chronicle*. He lived in the offices and was spoiled rotten and as fat as butter. 'This is a bit of a rush isn't it. The wedding isn't until the weekend. What'll Emily do without us?'

'It was the only flight I could get us on this week. Jake's staying on for a few more days.' He grinned. 'And I volunteered Cal. He's rounding up some extra hands. Oh, and Jake has told Aunt Lucy that the interview is on hold for a couple of weeks.'

'Weeks? I thought we were going for the weekend.'

'It's a long way to go for a weekend and you won't be starting work until next month.'

'No…'

'So I said you'd call her when you get back.' He put the tickets on the counter, lifted their bags onto the scale. 'That you'll make her famous.' He glanced back when she didn't answer. 'Or wasn't Toby Townsend that keen on the countryside issue?'

Oh, he'd been interested. Not in the issues, but he'd practically salivated at the thought of serialising Aunt Lucy's sensational revelations about half a century of life beneath the sheets in a quiet English village. His angle had certainly been 'different' from hers. He wanted all the scandals, all the secrets; she was supposed to befriend the old lady, gain her confidence, extract every last, juicy detail. It would be like taking candy from a baby. Unfortunately she would never be able to look herself in the mirror again. Big time. Big mistake.

'The clerk is waiting, Mike.'

'Willow, is something wrong?'

'No.' She glanced behind, anywhere rather than meet those clear, sharp eyes. 'There's a queue.' Mike followed her gaze, shrugged and gave his full attention to the check-in clerk.

She'd said, no. Nothing wrong. But as she stood there she began to wonder uneasily if she was being a little overconfident. Okay, she hadn't mentioned the name of the village, but she'd been talking to Toby's assistant over coffee; she'd mentioned the cottages, the Trust. It wouldn't take a man of his resources long to put it all together. Or to find someone else to do his dirty work.

She'd thought she was joining a respected newspaper, not one about to indulge in a circulation war and with its sights set firmly on the gutter.

She should warn Lucy, put her on her guard. No, that was hopeless, the sweet old dear would never understand. She needed to warn Jake. He'd know what to do.

'Mike, do you need me for this? I've been cross-legged all the way from South Kensington. I really need to visit the Ladies.'

'Since South Ken?' He grinned. 'No wonder you look stressed. I'll see you upstairs at passport control.' Then, suddenly, he said, 'Willow?'

'Don't worry, sweetheart, I'm not going to run out on you. This is Crysse's wedding, not mine.'

'Well, thanks. I think.'

She raced to the Ladies, searched her bag for the scrap of paper Jake had written his number on. Keyed it in with shaky fingers.

'Willow? I thought you were supposed to be on your way to the West Indies right now.'

'Boarding in twenty minutes. Look, I need to tell you something.'

He listened without interruption until she'd finished, then said, 'Don't worry. Aunt Lucy needs a holiday, I'll get someone to cover this place for a few weeks. Oh, and Willow—good luck for the big day.'

'Er, thanks.'

She hung up. Now her only problem would be in

convincing Mike that she hadn't given up her 'chance of a lifetime' for him.

After her dramatic last minute 'I want a career more than marriage' dash for freedom, abandoning him... Okay, so she hadn't *actually* abandoned him, he hadn't been there to be abandoned, but that was just luck and good timing. But she'd abandoned her wedding, her family, three hundred wedding guests and a cake big enough to feed five thousand. After that, he was going to find it pretty hard to believe she'd give it all up for one old lady she'd met for the first time yesterday.

Somehow she'd have to convince him that Toby had changed his mind. That he didn't have a use for a features writer whose imagination stretched no further than the village pump.

CHAPTER NINE

'WHAT are you going to wear?'

Crysse, having talked non-stop for about an hour, bubbling over with excitement and happiness, full of plans for her wedding, finally drew breath and paused expectantly. She was waiting for Willow's version of what had happened on Saturday. All the details. Including how they'd got back together. And if they were together, why they had separate rooms.

Her cousin would have to ask Mike about that. He'd made the booking. She suspected he was saying, Marry me or sleep alone. Maybe he hoped the hot tropical nights would bring her to her knees.

She was already there. She'd pulled her world down around her ears and was having to live with the consequences. No wedding. No big job. And Mike turning her own argument back on her.

But there was no way she was raining on Crysse's parade. Or risking her telling Mike. Hence the swift interjection.

'Have you bought a dress?' she asked when Crysse didn't immediately answer.

'Not yet. I decided to wait until you arrived. I thought we'd take a trip into town first thing tomorrow.' The ecstatic bride-to-be allowed herself to be distracted, but her look suggested that it was a temporary reprieve.

'Great.' Then, because the conversation seemed to

have stalled, Willow asked, 'Where did Sean say he was taking Mike?' The pair of them had taken off the minute Mike had dumped his bag in the room next door.

'They've probably gone to book a boat or something. Sean's been dying to try his hand at big-game fishing but there was no way I was getting involved…' Crysse checked her watch. 'I expect they're down in the bar right now, waiting for us to join them.'

'Sounds good to me. And you can tell me exactly what's happening. When are Aunt Grace and Uncle Jack arriving?'

'On Friday… Look, there's the wedding gazebo… Isn't it romantic… Everything fixed?' she broke off to ask Sean as they joined the two men beneath the thatched canopy of the poolside bar.

He grinned, kissed her cheek, whispered something so that Crysse giggled.

Willow exchanged a glance with Mike, then walked away to lean over the balustrade, looking out to sea. 'Tired?' Mike asked, joining her.

'A bit.' A lot. She'd attempted to sleep on the plane, more to avoid conversation, avoid Mike's questions about the new job, avoid thinking, than because she was tired. But now it was all catching up with her.

'Try and keep going, have a little something to eat. It'll help you with the time difference.'

'I know that,' she snapped.

'On the other hand,' he said slowly, 'maybe you'd be happier on your own.'

'No…yes… Maybe. I'm sorry, Mike. It's been a long day.'

He reached up, pushed his fingers through her hair, held it back and kissed her forehead. 'Don't apologise. I'll come and get you at dawn for a swim.'

'That sounds good.' She stood there with him for a moment, not wanting to leave him, wanting him to come with her. She didn't suggest it—a girl could only take so much rejection. He'd picked a fine moment to be high-minded about living together. She needed him so much, but how could she possibly say she'd marry him now? 'It's probably the only chance I'll get,' she said with a rueful smile. 'Crysse wants me to help her choose her dress tomorrow.'

'That'll be fun.'

'Of course it will.' She'd make sure nothing spoiled Crysse's big day. 'And you can enjoy your men's day out fishing.'

'Fishing?'

'Isn't that what you and Sean have planned for tomorrow? Just make sure he doesn't fall overboard, hmm?'

'I think I can manage that.' He kissed her again and then let her go. 'Goodnight, sweetheart.' Then, as she turned to go, he asked, 'Have you called your mother, let her know you've arrived safely? I've still got your phone.' Their cellphones had had to go through the X-ray equipment at the airport security check and he'd picked them both up, stowed them in his hand luggage. 'I'll come and get it for you if you like.'

And leave her at the bedroom door? 'No need. I called her on the room phone when I arrived.'

*   *   *

Maybe it was the fact that it was days since she'd slept in a bed, maybe her mind just took pity on her and shut down, but she was gone the instant her head hit the pillow.

She woke to a knock, the suffused light of predawn turning the ceiling gold, and for a moment she was happy. Then the knock came again. And memory disillusioned her.

'Willow? Are you awake?' She lay there for a moment, thinking about swimming with Mike, their bodies close, touching, wondering if she could bear it.

If she didn't answer, he'd go away. Maybe that would be best.

Mike waited for a moment, his fist laid against the locked door. If Willow was asleep he didn't want to disturb her. But something told him that she was lying there, wide awake and miserable; that he'd messed up again.

Until now, he'd never doubted that she loved him. Even though she hadn't made it to the church, it had never been about that. He'd thought keeping his distance was the answer, that once she'd seen Crysse, her enthusiasm for marriage would be rekindled.

Maybe he was kidding himself. Yesterday, on the plane, it had been obvious that she didn't want to talk about her job. He'd thought she was just trying to sort it all out in her mind. Maybe she was. Perhaps the realisation of just how big it was going to be, how her career was going to take off, had given her pause for thought.

Was she just waiting until Crysse and Sean were safely married to tell him that they had no future?

He lifted his hand from the door and left her to sleep. Maybe it was time he did some thinking of his own, stopped playing games and told her that she was more important to him than anything else in the entire world. That whatever she wanted was okay by him. Just as long as she wanted *him*.

'She really doesn't know?'

They'd spent the entire morning sorting out paperwork with local officials. Sean had already done it once so he knew exactly where to go. Now they were ready for a drink. Mike ordered, then answered the question.

'No. And don't tell Crysse for heaven's sake. I'm beginning to think this was a serious mistake. If it all goes pear-shaped, I'd rather Willow never knew.'

'Don't you think she might put two and two together when her parents arrive, when your parents arrive?'

'They're staying at a different hotel.'

'I've been to a surprise party before, but a surprise wedding sounds very risky. When exactly are you planning on telling the bride that this is going to be a double wedding?'

He'd thought it would be easy once they were in paradise. He was beginning to realise that it might take more than sunshine and a few palm trees to work the magic. 'I thought I'd wait until the jet lag wore off before I broached the subject,' he said.

'In other words, mind my own business.'

Mike shook his head. 'You're giving up a chunk of your holiday to help me sort out the paperwork—that makes it your business. And right now I'd welcome any suggestions from a man who seems to have got it right.'

'I had a moonlit beach and the sure and certain knowledge that Crysse was going to say yes.'

'Lucky man.'

'Yes, I am. And so will you be. Go for it. Everything is done.' He paused. 'Except the trip to the fish market. We need some large and fiercesome specimen with which to convince the ladies that we fished until we dropped.'

'Do we? Couldn't we just say we threw them back?'

Sean grinned. 'I know fishermen are supposed to tell tall tales, Mike, but whoever'd believe a story like that?'

'Maybe you've got a point—' His phone began to ring. 'That'll be Willow's father with details of their flight,' he said, taking out the phone, flipping it open.

He'd pressed receive before he realised that it wasn't his phone. That he'd picked up Willow's phone by mistake. A man's voice was saying, 'Hullo? Willow?' A voice he recognised.

'No, Jake,' he said grimly, 'this is Mike Armstrong. Would you mind telling me—?'

'Mike! Great. Look, will you tell Willow that everything is sorted? I've taken Aunt Lucy to stay with a friend for a couple of weeks. Panic over.'

Panic? What panic? 'What panic, Jake?'

'She didn't tell you?'

'We've been busy. Why don't you tell me exactly what panic is over?' he invited. 'And just why you're phoning Willow in the Caribbean to reassure her?'

*   *   *

'Are you going to tell me what happened?'

Crysse had been easy to distract during their shopping trip, but now the dress was hanging in Willow's wardrobe out of the sight of the groom-to-be and they were drinking iced tea in the shade of the poolside bar.

But it was fine.

She'd had plenty of time to work out what she was going to say. The hilariously weird tale of them meeting up at the motorway services took ages. Then the extraordinary notion of them both—independently—having the same idea of a place to hide out.

Her cousin obligingly laughed, exclaimed in all the right places, but was clearly less than convinced. 'Okay, that's the version for public consumption. When you feel like telling me what really happened, I'll be here with the shoulder to cry on.' Then, before Willow could deny there was another version, Crysse shrieked. 'What on earth is that?'

Stepping out from behind Willow, Sean grinned. 'A fish.' She pulled a face. 'I thought we might have it grilled for dinner.'

'Think again.'

'Where's Mike?' Willow asked.

'He's just taking a shower, he'll be down in a minute. And now I've given my beloved proof of my abilities as a hunter, I'm going to deliver this to the hotel kitchen and follow his example.'

'You do that. But next time check out the frozen-food department in the supermarket,' Crysse called after him. 'The fish there don't have whiskers.'

'Actually,' Willow said quickly, 'I think maybe I'll

take a shower, too. And maybe take a nap before dinner. My body clock is totally out of sync.'

Crysse still looked unimpressed. 'I'll tell Mike shall I? Or will he know you're avoiding him?'

'I'm not—'

'Puh-lease, darling. Treat me like an idiot if you must, but don't expect me to play along.' She peered over the top of her dark glasses. 'You messed up your own wedding, sweetie, but I'm warning you, do anything to spoil mine and you're cats' meat.'

Willow unlocked her door and let herself in, leaning back against it, breathless from her haste to avoid seeing Mike. Facing the questions he wasn't asking. Yet.

The room was cool, the curtains billowing in the breeze off the ocean. She frowned. She hadn't left the French doors open. Anyone could walk in.

Anyone had.

'Mike.'

'Willow,' he responded from the bed, where he was stretched out, hands behind his head, ankles crossed.

'How did you get in?'

'Does it matter?'

'No, I suppose not. I thought you were taking a shower. Going down for a drink—'

'That's what I told Sean. I wanted to check whether I was being paranoid, or whether you really were avoiding me. Now I know. Why didn't you tell me?'

'Tell you?'

'This could be a very long conversation. Or it could be a short one. Shall we try for brevity, since there's rather a lot to get through?'

'Mike—'

'I'll make it easy for you, shall I? I'll ask the questions, you can give me the answers. Tell me about your job.'

'You know—'

'Or maybe I should say about your *not* having a job. About the fact that you told Toby Townsend what he could do with his precious job when you understood what it entailed.'

She felt the blood drain from her face. Felt faint, dizzy. 'Who've you been talking to?'

'Jake. I picked up your phone by mistake this morning…' He'd been going to say, unfortunately, but couldn't quite bring himself to do that. From his point of view it had been a very fortunate mistake '…which is why he got me instead of you. He wanted you to know that Aunt Lucy is out of harm's way.'

'Thank goodness for that.'

'So we come to question number two.' He swung his feet off the bed. 'Why didn't you tell me?' he asked, advancing on her. She took a step back. 'About the *Globe*…' She took another. 'About Aunt Lucy…' She was running out of room to retreat. 'About Toby Townsend…' Her back was against the wall and his fingers caught at a stray curl, tucked it away behind her ear. Leaving her face exposed. Vulnerable. Her skin burning where he'd touched her. There was nowhere left to hide.

She shook her head. 'I c-couldn't.'

'Haven't you learned a thing, Willow? That secrets are corrosive. They eat away at a relationship until the foundations give way and suddenly there's nothing left.' She murmured something that he didn't quite catch. 'What?' Hoped he'd misheard. 'What did you say?'

'I was ashamed,' she whispered.

'Ashamed?' The sureness, the certainty of rightness in his voice wavered. 'What on earth have you got to be ashamed about?'

'I was prepared to throw it all away...' The sun had blushed her cheeks a brighter pink, but beneath the colour, she was chalk-white. 'The man I loved, my job on a terrific newspaper, a paper with heart and soul, and all for the cheap gratification of a step up the career ladder on a sleaze sheet that isn't fit to wrap potato peelings in—'

'Willow, please—'

'You warned me—no heart, you said—but I thought I knew better. Well, I know now. I know nothing.' She dashed away a half-formed tear, refusing to let it slide down her cheek. Self-pity would be the final humiliation. 'Talk about pride going before a fall...'

'Not a fall. Anything but a fall. Walking away was the big thing to do, Willow. And I wouldn't have expected anything less from you.'

'Really?' She sniffed, tried on a smile for size and decided it fitted. 'Do you think the *Maybridge Weekly Gazette* would take me on as a junior? If I promised to make the tea? I could work my way back up and by the time I'm forty they might take me seriously enough to let me loose on the local village news round-up—'

His hand covered her mouth. 'I take you seriously. I take you very seriously indeed. And I think you could look a lot higher than the *Maybridge Weekly Gazette*.'

'Been there, done that. I'm happier down in the foothills—'

'There's going to be a vacancy at the *Chronicle*. Maybe you should go for that.'

'Apply for my old job?' She shook her head. 'You can't go back. Never go back. Besides, Julie's been waiting to step into my shoes ever since we announced our engagement.'

'Has she? What made her think there'd be a vacancy? You had no plans to leave. Not until—'

'She assumed that marriage would be swiftly followed by maternity.'

'Oh, right. Well, it would be really unkind to disappoint her.' She looked up, her eyes for moment alight with hope. Did he mean what she thought he meant? 'It'll have to be another job, then.' Idiot! Why would he think anything of the sort?

It was cruel to tease her, Mike knew. Especially when he'd seen everything he needed to know in that look. The way her face had crumpled when he hadn't leapt in to fulfil the hope that had lit up her eyes like neon.

'Of course there is another post vacant at the *Chronicle*.' He stroked her heated cheeks with the tips of his fingers. 'And one of us should have a proper job, don't you think?'

She ignored that. She wasn't being drawn into that trap twice. 'What vacancy?'

'Dad is still looking for someone to take over from him.'

She stiffened, finally moved from the protection of

the wall. 'Not you!' she said urgently. 'You mustn't do it. Please, promise me, Mike!'

He drew a cross over his heart with the tip of his finger. 'You have my word. But you see there's only one other person who'll fit the bill.'

'Who?' She tried to think. 'Cal? Would he be interested?'

'Not Cal, sweetheart. You.' For a moment she stared at him, uncomprehending.

'But—but I don't know the first thing about running a newspaper.'

'Yes, you do. You proved it yesterday. The first thing is heart. Anyone can add up the figures. The rest is details. And Dad's quite happy to stick around until you've got those licked.'

'You've spoken to him?' She couldn't believe it.

'An hour ago.'

'And he really thinks... But, Mike, what about his determination that it'll be a family business...?' She shook her head. 'No, no. He just thinks this is the another way of getting you back—'

'Maybe he does.' His father, after all, was an incurable optimist. 'We know differently. But I should have known you'd spot the one snag in the whole arrangement.' He reached out, cradled her face in his hands, thumbed away the tears. 'He's got his heart set on an Armstrong at the helm, someone to carry the company on and pass it down to the next generation. If you want the job, love, I'm afraid you're going to have to marry me first.'

She looked up into his dear face. Saw the crinkle of laughter lines forming around his eyes, the fleeting appearance of a cleft in his cheek that on childhood photographs had been a dimple.

'Michael Armstrong, is that the most convoluted example of a marriage proposal ever promulgated?'

'Undoubtedly.' He grinned. 'So? Was that the most excruciating acceptance in the annals of romance?'

'It could certainly do with some editing. Shall we try again?'

'Will you marry me?'

'Yes,' she said. 'Please.'

He grinned. 'Such lovely manners. Your mother would be proud of you.' She responded with a word calculated to raise her mother's eyebrows and blood pressure. 'Mmm. Well, now that's settled you'd better have this back.' He produced her ring from his shirt pocket, the diamond flashing in the sunlight as he slipped it on her finger.

'I think you should kiss me before I cry.'

'I intend to do a lot more than that, my love. But there's just one more thing we have to settle. About the wedding.'

'Oh, lord,' she wailed. 'Couldn't we just run away somewhere?'

'I thought we already had. I thought perhaps we could make it a double celebration on Saturday.'

'Saturday? With Crysse? Oh, my… But what about—'

'Your parents and mine will be arriving tomorrow morning. Your mother is bringing your dress. Sean and I have spent all day fixing up the paperwork.'

Willow opened her mouth on a silent, 'oh'. Then she said, 'You…' He waited. 'You did that before you knew about the job, didn't you?'

'Optimism must run in the family.'

'I love optimism. And I love you, Michael. I'd live with you in a hut and eat seaweed, do you know that?'

'The way you cook? I don't think so. Let's try the hayloft for a while,' he said, kissing her lightly on the mouth. 'Until maternity sends us looking for somewhere larger—'

'Maternity?'

'Didn't I mention that bit? You not only have to run the newspaper, you'll also have to provide the next generation.'

'It looks as if I'm going to be busy.'

'Count on it. But don't worry, I'm more than happy to help out with that part of the plan.'

'That sounds promising. But when you said looking for somewhere larger—'

'When I said larger, I meant, just large enough,' he promised. 'For us, and the next generation, and the goldfish and the cuddly toys...' And this time, when he kissed her, he made it very clear that the time for talking was over.

Willow and Mike and Crysse and Sean lined up in a white gazebo decked with tropical flowers, beneath the setting sun. No bridesmaids, the minimum of ribbons, the only guests their immediate families and passing holiday-makers who paused to enjoy the special occasion.

There was a toast, but no speeches by request and, as soon as they could escape, Mike took Willow for a barefoot walk along the beach in the moonlight, his cream linen trousers rolled up over his ankles, her lovely gown brushing the sand behind her.

When they reached a small jetty, he led her along it to a boat, tied up alongside. The owner looked up and grinned out of his ebony face, before starting the engine.

'Shall we go?' Mike said.

'Go?' Willow asked, startled. 'Go where?'

He grinned, bent to kiss the smooth skin behind her ear, and then swept her up into his arms. 'A double wedding is one thing, my darling, but I have no intention of sticking around to share my honeymoon with the in-laws. I've rented us a cottage along the coast for the next couple of weeks.'

'But—' She glanced back along the beach.

'Any objections?'

'No, it's just…well, I'll need more than a wedding dress for the next week.'

'Will you?' Mike grinned as he set her down on the deck. 'Whatever gave you that idea?'

Willow shook her head, laughed as she spotted their suitcases standing in the cabin. 'You're getting good at this running away thing.'

'Improving,' he agreed. 'This time the groom and the bride are running away together.' Mike's eyes were level with hers and her breath caught in her throat.

Willow reached up, touched his face with her fingertips. 'Together is the best word I know,' she murmured as she followed them with her lips. 'It doesn't get any better than that.'

In March 2001,

presents the next book in

DIANA PALMER's

enthralling *Soldiers of Fortune* trilogy:

THE WINTER SOLDIER

Cy Parks had a reputation around Jacobsville for his taciturn and solitary ways. But spirited Lisa Monroe wasn't put off by the mesmerizing mercenary, and drove him to distraction with her sweetly tantalizing kisses. Though he'd never admit it, Cy was getting mighty possessive of the enchanting woman who needed the type of safeguarding only he could provide. But who would protect the beguiling beauty from *him...?*

Soldiers of Fortune...prisoners of love.

Silhouette®

Where love comes alive™

Available only from Silhouette Desire at your favorite retail outlet.

Visit Silhouette at
www.eHarlequin.com

SDWS

PARENTS WANTED

Families in the making!

In the orphanage of a small Australian town
called Bay Beach are little children desperately
in need of love, and dreaming of their very
own family....

The answer to their dreams can also be found
in Bay Beach! Couples who are destined for
each other—even if they don't know it yet.
Brought together by love for these tiny
children, can they find true love themselves—
and finally become a real family?

Titles in this series by fan-favorite
MARION LENNOX are

A Child in Need—(April HR #3650)
Their Baby Bargain—(July HR #3662)

Look out for further Parents Wanted stories
in Harlequin Romance®, coming soon!

Available wherever Harlequin Books are sold.

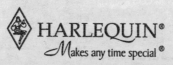

HARLEQUIN®
Makes any time special ®

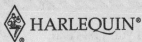

HARLEQUIN®

makes any time special—online...

eHARLEQUIN.com

your romantic escapes

—Indulgences—
- Monthly guides to indulging yourself, such as:
  - ★ Tub Time: A guide for bathing beauties
  - ★ Magic Massages: A treat for tired feet

—Horoscopes—
- Find your daily Passionscope, weekly Lovescopes and Erotiscopes
- Try our compatibility game

—Reel Love—
- Read all the latest romantic movie reviews

—Royal Romance—
- Get the latest scoop on your favorite royal romances

—Romantic Travel—
- For the most romantic destinations, hotels and travel activities